PUFFIN BOOKS
THE ADVENTURES OF FELUDA
THE INCIDENT ON THE KALKA MAIL

Satyajit Ray (1921-1992) was one of the greatest filmmakers of his time, renowned for films like *Pather Panchali, Charulata, Aranyer Din Ratri* and *Ghare Baire*. He was awarded the Oscar for Lifetime Achievement by the Academy of Motion Picture Arts and Science in 1992, and in the same year, was also honoured with the Bharat Ratna.

Ray was also a writer of repute, and his short stories, novellas, poems and articles, written in Bengali, have been immensely popular ever since they first began to appear in the children's magazine *Sandesh* in 1961. Among his most famous creations are the master sleuth Feluda and the scientist Professor Shonku.

*

Gopa Majumdar has translated several works from Bengali to English, the most notable of these being Ashapurna Debi's *Subarnalata* and Bibhutibhushan Bandyopadhyay's *Aparajito*, for which she won the Sahitya Akademi Award in 2001. She has translated several volumes of Satyajit Ray's short stories and all of the Feluda stories for Penguin Books India. She is currently translating Ray's Professor Shonku stories, which are forthcoming in Puffin.

Read the other Adventures of Feluda in Puffin

THE ADVENTURES OF FELUDA

THE INCIDENT ON THE KALKA MAIL

Satyajit Ray

Translated from the Bengali by Gopa Majumdar

PUFFIN BOOKS

PUFFIN BOOKS

Penguin Books India (P) Ltd., 11 Community Centre, Panchsheel Park, New Delhi
110 017, India

Penguin Books Ltd., 80 Strand, London WC2R 0RL, UK

Penguin Group Inc., 375 Hudson Street, New York, NY 10014, USA

Penguin Books Australia Ltd., 250 Camberwell Road, Camberwell, Victoria 3124,
Australia

Penguin Books Canada Ltd., 10 Alcorn Avenue, Suite 300, Toronto, Ontario M4V
3B2, Canada

Penguin Books (NZ) Ltd., Cnr Rosedale and Airborne Roads, Albany, Auckland,
New Zealand

Penguin Books (South Africa) (Pty) Ltd, 24 Sturdee Avenue, Rosebank 2196, South
Africa

This edition first published in Puffin by Penguin Books India 2004
Copyright © The Estate of Satyajit Ray 2004
This translation copyright © Penguin Books India 2004

Typeset in Garamond by Mantra Virtual Services, New Delhi
Printed at Thomson Press, Noida

CHAPTER 1

I had only just finished reading a hair-raising account of an expedition by Captain Scott. Who knew I would have to travel to the land of mist and snow so soon after this? Well no, I don't mean the North or the South Pole. I don't think Feluda would ever be required to help solve mysteries in such remote corners. The place I am talking about is in our own country. Here I saw snowflakes floating down from the sky like cotton fluff. It spread on the ground like a carpet, dazzling my eyes as the sun fell on it; yet it stayed soft enough to be scooped and gathered into a ball.

This particular adventure started last March, on a Thursday morning. By this time, Feluda had become fairly well known as a detective, so his number of clients had grown. But he didn't accept a case unless it was one that gave him the chance to sharpen his remarkable brain. When I first heard about this case, it did not strike me as anything extraordinary. But Feluda must have sensed a great challenge, which was why he agreed so readily. The only other factor that might have influenced his decision was that the client seemed to be pretty well off, so perhaps he was expecting a fat fee. However, when I mentioned this to Feluda, he gave me such a glare that I had to shut up immediately.

The client was called Dinanath Lahiri. He rang us in the evening on Wednesday and made an appointment for eight o' clock the following morning. On the dot of eight on Thursday, we heard a car stop and blow its horn outside our house in Tara Road. The horn sounded strangely different from other cars. I sprang to my feet and moved towards the door, but Feluda stopped me with a gesture.

'You must learn,' he said, 'to play it cool. At least wait till the bell rings.'

It rang in a few seconds. When I opened the door, the first thing I saw was a huge car. Never before had I seen such a big car, except for a Rolls-Royce. The gentleman who emerged from it was equally impressive, though that had nothing to do with his size. A man in his mid-fifties, he had a remarkably fair complexion and was wearing a fine dhoti and kurta. On his feet were white nagras with an upturned front. In his left hand was a walking-stick with an ivory handle; and in his right hand he held a blue square attaché case, of a type which I had seen many times before. There were two in our own house—one was Baba's, the other belonged to Feluda. They were handed out by Air-India as free gifts to their passengers.

Feluda offered the gentleman the most comfortable armchair in the living-room and took an ordinary chair himself to sit opposite him.

'I rang last night,' said our visitor. 'My name is Dinanath Lahiri.'

Feluda cleared his throat and said, 'Before you say anything further, may I ask you a couple of questions?'

'Of course.'

'First of all, would you mind having a cup of tea?'

Mr Lahiri folded his hands, bent his head politely and replied, 'You must forgive me, Mr Mitter, I am not used to having anything except at certain hours. But please don't let me stop you from having a cup of tea, if you so wish.'

'All right. My second question is—is your car a Hispano Suiza?'

'Yes, that's right. There aren't too many of those in this country. My father bought it in 1934. Are you interested in cars?'

Feluda smiled, 'Yes, among other things. But my interests are chiefly related to my profession.'

'I see. Allow me now to tell you why I'm here. You may find the whole thing totally insignificant. I am aware of your reputation, so there's no way I can insist that you take the case. I can only make a request.'

There was a certain polish and sophistication in his voice and the way he spoke, but not even the slightest trace of arrogance. On the contrary, Mr Lahiri spoke gently and quietly.

'Let's hear the details of your case,' said Feluda.

'You may call it my case,' said Mr Lahiri with a smile, pointing at the blue object in his hand, 'or the tale of

3

my attaché case . . . ha ha. You see, my story revolves round this attaché case.'

Feluda glanced at the case and said, 'It seems to have gone abroad few times. The tags are torn but I can see the elastic bands on the handle—one, two, three, four . . .'

'Yes, the handle of my own case also has elastic bands hanging from it.'

'Your own case? You mean this one isn't yours?'

'No. This belongs to someone else. It got exchanged with mine.'

'I see. Where did this happen? In a plane, or was it a train?'

'It was a train. Kalka Mail. I was coming back from Delhi. There were four passengers in a first class compartment, including myself. My attaché case must have got mixed up with one of the other three.'

'I assume you do not know whose it was . . . ?'

'No. If I did, I don't suppose I'd need your help.'

'And you don't know the names of the others?'

'There was another Bengali. His name was Pakrashi. He travelled from Delhi, like me.'

'How did you get to know his name?'

'One of the other passengers happened to recognize him. I heard this other man say, "Hello, Mr Pakrashi!" and then they got talking. I think both were businessmen. I kept hearing words like contract and tender.'

'You didn't learn the name of this other man?'

'No. He was not a Bengali, though he was speaking the language quite well. I gathered he came from Simla.'

'And the fourth passenger?'

'He stayed on one of the upper berths most of the time. I saw him climb down only during lunch and dinner. He was not a Bengali, either. He offered me an apple soon after we left Delhi and said it was from his own orchard. So perhaps he was from Simla, too.'

'Did you eat that apple?'

'Yes, certainly. It was a good, tasty apple.'

'So you don't mind eating things outside your regular hours when you're in a train?'

Mr Lahiri burst out laughing.

'My God! I'd never have thought you'd pick that up! But you're right. In a moving train I am tempted to break my own rules.'

'OK,' said Feluda, 'I now need to know exactly where who was sitting.'

'I was on a lower berth. Mr Pakrashi was on the berth above mine. On the other side, the man who gave me the apple sat on the upper berth and below him was the businessman who knew Mr Pakrashi.'

Feluda was silent for a few moments. Then he rubbed his hands together and said, 'If you don't mind, I am going to ask for some tea. Do have a cup if you want. Topshe, would you please go in?'

I ran in to tell our cook, Srinath, to bring the tea. When I returned, Feluda had opened the attaché case.

'Wasn't it locked?' he asked.

'No. Nor was mine. So whoever took it could easily have seen what was in it. This one is full of routine, ordinary stuff.'

True. It contained little besides two English dailies, a cake of soap, a comb, a hairbrush, a toothbrush, toothpaste, a shaving kit, a handkerchief and a paperback.

'Did your case contain anything valuable?' Feluda wanted to know.

'No, nothing. In fact, what my case had was probably of less value than what you see here. The only interesting thing in it was a manuscript. It was a travelogue, about Tibet. I had taken it with me to read on the train. It made very good reading.'

'A travelogue about Tibet?' Feluda was now clearly curious.

'Yes. It was written in 1917 by a Shambhucharan Bose. As far as I can make out, my uncle must have brought it, since it was dedicated to him. His name was Satinath Lahiri. He had lived in Kathmandu for many years, working as a private tutor in the household of the Ranas. He returned home about forty-five years ago, a sick old man. In fact, he died shortly after his return. Among his belongings was a Nepali box. It lay in a corner of our box room. We had all forgotten its existence until recently, when I called the Pest Control. The room had to be emptied for the men to work in. It was then that I found the box and, in it, the manuscript.'

'When did this happen?'

'The day before I left for Delhi.'

Feluda grew a little thoughtful. 'Shambhucharan?' he muttered to himself. 'Shambhucharan . . . Shambhucharan . . .'

'Anyway,' continued Mr Lahiri, 'that manuscript does not mean very much to me. To tell you the truth, I wasn't really interested in getting my attaché case back. Besides, there was no guarantee that I would find the owner of the one that got exchanged with mine. So I gave this case to my nephew. But since last night, I have been thinking. These articles that you see before you may not be expensive, but for their owner they might have a great deal of sentimental value. Look at this handkerchief, for instance. It's initialled "G". Someone had embroidered the letter with great care. Who could it be? His wife? Perhaps she is no more. Who knows? Shouldn't I try to return this attaché case to its rightful owner? I was getting worried, so I took it back from my nephew and came to you. Frankly, I don't care if my own case does not come back to me. I would simply feel a lot more comfortable if this one could be restored to whoever owns it.'

Srinath came in with the tea. Feluda, of late, had become rather fussy about his tea. What he was now going to drink had come from the Makaibari tea estate of Kurseong. Its fragrance filled the room the instant Srinath placed the cups before us. Feluda took a sip quietly and said, 'Did you have to open your case quite a few times in the train?'

'No, not at all. I opened it only twice. I took the manuscript out soon after the train left Delhi, and then I put it back before going to sleep.'

Feluda lit a Charminar and blew out a couple of smoke rings.

'So you'd like me to return this case to its owner and get yours back for you—right?'

'Yes. But does that disappoint you? Do you think it's all a bit too tame?'

Feluda ran his fingers through his hair. 'No,' he said, 'I understand your sentiments. And I must admit that your case is different from the ones I usually

7

handle.'

Dinanath Babu looked visibly relieved. 'Your acceptance means a lot to me,' he said, letting out a deep breath.

'I shall, of course, do my best,' Feluda replied, 'but I cannot guarantee success. You must understand that. However, I should now like some information.'

'Yes?'

Feluda rose quickly and went into the next room. He returned with his famous blue notebook. Then, pencil in hand, he began asking questions.

'When did you leave Delhi?'

'On 5 March at 6.30 p.m. I reached Calcutta the next morning at nine-thirty.'

'Today is the 9th. So you arrived here three days ago, and you rang me yesterday.'

Feluda opened the attaché case and took out a yellow Kodak film container. As he unscrewed its lid, a few pieces of betel-nut fell out of it on the table. Feluda put one of these in his mouth and resumed speaking.

'Was there anything in your case that might give one an idea of your name and address?'

'No, not as far as I can recall.'

'Hm. Could you now please describe your fellow passengers?'

Dinanath Babu tilted his head and stared at the ceiling, frowning a little.

'Pakrashi would have been about the same age as me. Between sixty and sixty-five. He had salt-and-pepper hair, brushed back. He wore glasses and his voice was rather harsh.'

'Good.'

'The man who offered me the apple had a fair complexion. He was tall and slim, had a sharp nose, wore gold-framed glasses and was quite bald except for a few strands of black hair around his ears. He spoke to me only in English, with a flawless accent. And he had a cold. He kept blowing his nose into a tissue.'

'A pukka sahib, I see! And the third gentleman?'

'His appearance was really quite ordinary—there was nothing that one might have noticed in particular. But he was the only one who ordered a vegetarian thali.'

Feluda jotted all this down in his notebook. Then he looked up and asked, 'Anything else?'

'No, I can't recall anything else worth reporting. You see, I spent most of the day reading. And I fell asleep soon after dinner. I don't usually sleep very well in a train. But this time I slept like a baby until we arrived at Howrah. In fact, it was Mr Pakrashi who woke me.'

'In that case, presumably you were the last person to leave the coach?'

'Yes.'

'By which time one of the other three had walked out with your attaché case?'

'Yes.'

'Hm,' Feluda said, shutting his notebook, 'I'll see what I can do.'

Dinanath Babu rose.

'I will, of course, pay your fee. But you will naturally need something to begin your investigation. I brought some cash today for this purpose.' He took out a white envelope from his pocket and offered it to Feluda, who took it coolly with a casual 'Oh, thanks' and stuffed it into his own pocket, together with his pencil.

Dinanath Babu came out and began walking towards his car. 'You will get my telephone number from the directory,' he said, 'please let me know if you hear anything. As a matter of fact, you can come straight to my house if need be. I am usually home in the evening.'

The yellow Hispano Suiza disappeared in the direction of Rashbehari Avenue, blowing its horn like a conch shell, startling all passers-by. We returned to the living-room. Feluda took the chair Dinanath Babu had occupied. Then he crossed his legs, stretched lazily and said, 'Another twenty-five years . . . and people with such an aristocratic style will have vanished.'

The blue case was still lying on the table. Feluda took its contents out one by one. Each object was really quite ordinary. Whoever bought them could not have spent more than fifty rupees.

'Let's make a list,' said Feluda. This was soon ready, and it contained the following:

Two English dailies from Delhi, neatly folded. One was the *Sunday Statesman*, the other the *Sunday Hindustan Times*.

A half-used tube of Binaca toothpaste. The empty portion had been rolled up.

A green Binaca toothbrush.

A Gillette safety razor.

Three thin Gillette blades in a packet.

An old and used Old Spice shaving cream. It was nearly finished.

A shaving brush.

A nail cutter—pretty old.

Three tablets of Aspro wrapped in a cellophane sheet.

A folded map of Calcutta. It measured 4' x 5' when opened.

A Kodak film container with chopped betel-nuts in it.

A matchbox, brand new.

A Venus red-and-blue pencil.

A white handkerchief, with the letter 'G' embroidered in one corner.

A pen-knife, possibly from Moradabad.

A small face-towel.

A rusted old safety-pin.

Three equally rusted paper clips.

A shirt button.

A detective novel—Ellery Queen's *The Door Between*.

Feluda picked up the book and turned a few pages.

'No, there's no mention of the owner's name,' he said, 'but he clearly had the habit of marking a page by folding its corner. There are 236 pages in this book. The last sign of folding is at page 212. I assume he finished reading it.'

Feluda now turned his attention to the handkerchief.

'The first letter of his name or surname must be "G". No, it must be his first name, that's far more natural.'

Then he opened the map of Calcutta and spread it on the table.

'Red marks,' he said, looking closely at it, 'someone marked it with a red pencil . . . hm . . . one, two, three, four, five . . . hm . . . Chowringhee . . . Park Street . . . I see. Topshe, get the telephone directory.'

Feluda put the map back into the case. Then he began turning the pages of the telephone directory. 'P . . . here we are,' he said. 'There are only sixteen Pakrashis listed here. Two of them are doctors, so we can easily leave them out.'

'Why?'

'The man who recognized him in the train called him Mr Pakrashi, not Doctor, remember?'

'Oh yes, that's right.'

Feluda picked up the telephone and began dialling. Each time he got through, I heard him say, 'Has Mr Pakrashi returned from Delhi? . . . Oh, sorry!'

This happened five times in a row. But the sixth number he dialled apparently got him the right man for, this time, he spoke for much longer. Then he said 'Thanks' and put the phone down.

'I think I've got him,' he said to me. 'N.C. Pakrashi. He answered the phone himself. He returned from Delhi by Kalka Mail the day before yesterday. Everything tallies, except that his luggage didn't get exchanged.'

'Then why did you make an appointment with him this evening?'

'Why, he can give us some information about the other passengers, can't he? He appears to be an ill-tempered fellow, but it would take more than ill-temper to put Felu Mitter off. Come, Topshe, let's go out.'

'Now? I thought we were meeting Mr Pakrashi in the evening?'

'Yes, but before calling on Pakrashi I think we need to visit your Uncle Sidhu. Now.'

CHAPTER 2

Uncle Sidhu was no relation. He used to be Baba's next door neighbour when he lived in our old ancestral home, long before I was born. Baba treated him like a brother, and we all called him Uncle. Uncle Sidhu's knowledge about most things was extraordinary and his memory remarkably powerful. Feluda and I both admired and respected him enormously.

But why did Feluda want to see him at this time? The first question Feluda asked made that clear. 'Have you heard of a travel writer called Shambhucharan Bose? He used to write in English, about sixty years ago.'

Uncle Sidhu's eyes widened.

'Good heavens, Felu, haven't you read his book on the Terai?'

'Oh yes,' said Feluda, 'now I do remember. The man's name sounded familiar, but no, I haven't read the book.'

'It was called *The Terrors of Terai*. A British publisher in London published it in 1915. Shambhucharan was both a traveller and a shikari. But by profession he was a doctor. He used to practise in Kathmandu. This was long before the present royal family came into power. The powerful people in Nepal then were the Ranas. Shambhucharan treated and cured a lot of ailments among the Ranas. He mentioned one of them in his book. Vijayendra Shamsher Jung Bahadur. The man was keen on hunting, but he drank very heavily. Apparently, he used to climb a machan with a bottle in one hand and a rifle in the other. But both his hands stayed steady when it came to pressing the trigger. Except once. Only once did he miss, and the tiger jumped up on the machan. It was Shambhucharan who shot the tiger from the next machan and saved the Rana's life. The Rana expressed his gratitude by giving him a priceless jewel. A most thrilling story. Try and get a copy from the National Library. I don't think you'll get it easily anywhere else.'

'Did he ever go to Tibet?'

'Yes, certainly. He died in 1921, soon after I finished college. I saw an obituary on him, I remember. It said he had gone to Tibet after his retirement, although he died in Kathmandu.'

'I see.'

Feluda remained silent for a few moments. Then he said, in a clear, distinct tone, 'Supposing an unpublished manuscript was discovered today, written after his visit to Tibet, would that be a valuable document?'

'My goodness!' Uncle Sidhu's bald dome glistened with excitement. 'You don't know what you're saying, Felu! Valuable? I still remember the very high praise Terai had received from the London *Times*. It wasn't just the stories he told, Shambhucharan's language was easy, lucid and clear as crystal. Why, have you found such a manuscript?'

'No, but there might be one in existence.'

'If you can lay your hands on it, please don't forget to show it to me, Felu. And in case it gets auctioned, let me know. I'd be prepared to bid up to five thousand rupees . . .'

We left soon after this, but not before two cups of cocoa had been pressed upon us.

'Mr Lahiri doesn't even know his attaché case contains such hot stuff,' I said as we came out. 'Aren't you going to tell him?'

'Wait. There's no need to rush things. Let's see where all this leads to. In any case, I have taken the job, haven't I? It's just that now I feel a lot more enthusiastic.'

Naresh Chandra Pakrashi lived in Lansdowne Road. It was obvious that his house had been built at least forty years ago. Feluda had taught me how to assess the age of a house. For instance, houses built fifty years ago had a certain type of window, which was different from those built ten years later. The railings on verandas and terraces, patterns on gates, pillars at porticos—all bore evidence of the period a building was made. This particular house must have been built in the 1920s.

The first thing I noticed as we climbed out of our taxi was a notice outside the main gate: 'Beware of the Dog'.

'It would have made better sense,' remarked Feluda, 'if it had said, "Beware of the Owner of the Dog".'

We passed through the gate and found a chowkidar standing near the porch. Feluda gave him his visiting card, which bore the legend: 'Pradosh C. Mitter, Private Investigator'. The chowkidar disappeared with the card and reappeared a few minutes later.

'Please go in,' he said.

We had to cross a wide marble landing before we got to the door of the living-room. It must have been about ten feet high. We lifted the curtain and walked in, to be greeted by rows and rows of books, all stashed in huge almirahs. There was quite a lot of other furniture, a wall-to-wall carpet, pictures on the walls, and even a chandelier. But the whole place had an unkempt air. Apparently, no one cared to clean it regularly.

We found Mr Pakrashi in his study, which was hidden behind the living-room. The sound of typing had already reached our ears. Now we saw a man sitting behind an ancient typewriter, which rested on a massive table, covered with green rexine. The table was placed on the right. On our left, as we stepped in, we saw three couches and a small round table. On this stood a chess board with all the chessmen in place, and a book on the game. The last thing my eyes fell on was a large dog, curled up and asleep in one corner of the room.

The man fitted Dinanath Babu's description. A pipe hung from his mouth. He stopped typing upon our entry, and his eyes swept over us both. 'Which one of you is Mr Mitter?' he finally asked.

Perhaps it was his idea of a joke, but Feluda did not laugh. He answered civilly enough, 'I am Pradosh Mitter. This is my cousin.'

'How was I to know?' said Mr Pakrashi. 'Little boys have gone into so many different things . . . music, acting, painting; why, some have even become religious gurus! So your cousin here might well have been the great sleuth himself. But anyway, tell me why you're here. What do you want from a man who's never done anything other than mind his own business?'

Feluda was right. If ever a competition was held in irascibility, this man would have been a world champion.

'Who did you say sent you here?' he wanted to know.

'Mr Lahiri mentioned your name. He arrived from Delhi three days ago. You and he travelled in the same compartment.'

'I see. And is he the one whose attaché case got lost?'

'Not lost. Merely mistaken for someone else's.'

'Careless fool. But why did he have to employ you to retrieve it? What precious object did it contain?'

'There was nothing much, really, except an old manuscript. There is no other copy.'

I could tell why Feluda mentioned the manuscript. If he told Mr Pakrashi the real reason why he had been employed, no doubt Mr Pakrashi would have laughed in derision.

'Manuscript?' he asked somewhat suspiciously.

'Yes. A travelogue written by Shambhucharan Bose.

Mr Lahiri had read it on the train, then put it back in the case.'

'Well, the man is not just a fool, he seems to be a liar, too. You see, although I had an upper berth, I spent most of the day sitting right next to him. He never read anything other than a newspaper and a Bengali magazine.'

Feluda did not say anything. Mr Pakrashi paused for breath, then continued, 'I don't know what you'd make of it as a sleuth. I find the whole thing distinctly suspicious. Anyway, if you wish to go on a wild-goose chase, suit yourself. I cannot offer any help. I told you on the phone I have about three of those Air-India bags, but on this trip I didn't take any with me.'

'One of the other passengers knew you, didn't he?'

'Who, Brijmohan? Yes. He is a moneylender. I've had a few dealings with him.'

'Could he have had a blue case?'

'How on earth should I know?' Mr Pakrashi frowned darkly.

'Could you give me Brijmohan's telephone number?'

'Look it up in the directory. S. M. Kedia & Co. SM was Brijmohan's father. Their office is in Lenin Sarani. And one more thing—you're wrong in thinking I knew only one of the other passengers. As a matter of fact, I knew two of them.'

'Who's the second one?' Feluda sounded surprised.

'Dinanath Lahiri. I had seen him before at the races. He used to be quite a lad. Now I believe he's changed his lifestyle and even found himself a guru in Delhi. Heaven knows if any of this is true.'

'What about the fourth man in your coach?' asked

Feluda. He was obviously trying to gain as much information as he could.

'What's going on?' shouted Mr Pakrashi, pulling a face, in spite of the pipe still hanging from his mouth. 'Are you here simply to ask questions? Am I an accused standing trial or what?'

'No, sir,' said Feluda calmly. 'I am asking these questions only because you play chess all by yourself, you clearly have a sharp brain, a good memory, and . . .'

Mr Pakrashi thawed a little. He cleared his throat and said, 'Chess has become an addiction. The partner I used to play with is no more. So now I play alone.'

'Every day?'

'Yes. Another reason for that is my insomnia. I play until about three in the morning.'

'Do you never take a pill to help you sleep?'

'I do sometimes. But it doesn't always help. Not that it matters. I go to bed at three, and rise at eight. Five hours is good enough at my age.'

'Is typing also . . . one of your addictions?' Feluda asked with his lopsided smile.

'No, but there are times when I do like to do my own typing. I have a secretary, who's pretty useless. Anyway, you were talking about the fourth passenger, weren't you? He had sharp features, was quite bald, a non-Bengali, spoke very good English and offered me an apple. I didn't eat it. What else would you like to know? I am fifty-three and my dog is three-and-a-half. He's a boxer and doesn't like visitors to stay for more than half an hour. So . . .'

'An interesting man,' Feluda remarked. We were out in the street, but not walking in the direction of home. Why Feluda chose to go in the opposite direction, I could not tell; nor did he make any attempt at hailing either of the two empty taxis that sailed by.

One little thing was bothering me. I had to mention it to Feluda.

'Didn't Dinanath Babu say he thought Pakrashi was about sixty? But Mr Pakrashi himself said he was fifty-three and, quite frankly, he didn't seem older than that. Isn't that funny?'

'All it proves is that Dinanath Babu's power of observation is not what it should be,' said Feluda.

A couple of minutes later, we reached Lower Circular Road. Feluda turned left. 'Are you going to look at that case of robbery?' I asked. Only three days ago, the papers had reported a case of a daylight robbery. Apparently, three masked men had walked into a jeweller's shop on Lower Circular Road and got away with a lot of valuable jewellery and precious stones, firing recklessly in the air as they made their escape in a black Ambassador car. 'It might be fun tracing those daredevils,' Feluda had said. But sadly, no one had come forward to ask him to investigate. So I thought perhaps he was going to ask a few questions on his own. But Feluda paid no attention to me. It seemed as though his sole purpose in life, certainly at that moment, was to get some exercise and so he would do nothing but continue to walk.

A little later, he turned left again rather abruptly, and walked briskly into the Hindustan International Hotel. I followed him quickly.

'Did anyone from Simla check in at your hotel on 6 March?' Feluda asked the receptionist, 'His first name starts with a "G" . . . I'm afraid I can't recall his full name.'

Neither Brijmohan nor Naresh Pakrashi had names that started with a 'G'. So this had to the applewalla.

The receptionist looked at his book.

'There are two foreigners listed here on 6 March,' he said, 'Gerald Pratley and G. R. Holmes. Both came from abroad.'

'Thank you,' said Feluda and left.

We took a taxi as we came out. 'Park Hotel,' Feluda said to the driver and lit a Charminar.

'If you had looked carefully at those red marks on the map,' he said to me, 'you'd have seen they were markers for hotels. It's natural that the man would want to stay at a good hotel. At present, there are five well-known hotels in Calcutta—Grand, Hindustan International, Park, Great Eastern and Ritz Continental. And those red marks had been placed on these. The Park Hotel would be our next port of call.'

As it turned out, no one with a name starting with 'G' had checked in at the Park on 6 March. But the Grand offered some good news. Feluda happened to know one of its Bengali receptionists called Dasgupta. He showed us their visitors' book. Only one Indian had checked in on the 6th. He did arrive from Simla and his name was G. C. Dhameeja.

'Is he still here?'

'No, sir. He checked out yesterday.'

The little flicker of hope in my mind was snuffed out immediately. Feluda, too, was frowning. But he didn't stop asking questions.

'Which room was he in?'

'Room 216.'

'Is it empty now?'

'Yes. We're expecting a guest this evening, but right now it's vacant.'

'Can I speak to the room boy?'

'Certainly. I'll get someone to show you the way.'

We took the lift up to the second floor. A walk down a long corridor finally brought us to room 216. The room boy appeared at this point. We went into the room with him. Feluda began pacing.

'Can you remember the man who left yesterday? He was staying in this room.'

'Yes, sir.'

'Now try to remember carefully. What luggage did he have?'

'A large suitcase, and a smaller one.'

'Was it blue?'

'Yes. When I came back to the room after filling his flask, I found him taking things out of the blue case. He seemed to be looking for something.'

'Very good. Can you remember if this man had a few apples—perhaps in a paper bag?'

'Yes. There were three apples. He took them out and kept them on a plate.'

'What did this man look like?'

But the description the room boy gave did not help. At least a hundred thousand men in Calcutta would have fitted that description.

However, there was reason to feel pleased. We now had the name and address of the man whose attaché case had got exchanged with Mr Lahiri's. Mr Dasgupta gave us a piece of paper as we went out. I glanced over Feluda's shoulder and saw what was written on it:

G. C. Dhameeja
'The Nook'
Wild Flower Hall
Simla

CHAPTER 3

'Kaka has gone out. He'll return around seven,' we were told.

So this was Dinanath Babu's nephew. We had come straight from the Grand Hotel to Dinanath Babu's house to report our progress, stopping on our way only to buy some meetha paan from a shop outside the New Empire.

Lined on one side of the gate of Mr Lahiri's house were four garages. Three of these were empty. The fourth contained an old, strange looking car. 'Italian,' said Feluda. 'It's a Lagonda.'

The chowkidar took our card in, but, instead of Dinanath Babu, a younger man emerged from the house. He couldn't have been more than thirty. Of medium height, he had fair skin like his uncle; his hair was long and tousled; and running down from his ears were broad sideburns, the kind that seemed to be all the rage among fashionable men. The man was staring hard at Feluda.

'Could we please wait until he returns?' asked Feluda. 'We have something rather important to discuss, you see.'

'Please come this way.'

We were taken into the living-room. The walls and the floor were littered with tiger and bear skins; a huge head of a buffalo graced the wall over the main door. Perhaps Dinanath Babu's uncle had been a shikari, too. May be that was why he and Shambhucharan had been so close?

'My uncle goes out for a walk every evening. He'll be back soon.'

Dinanath Babu's nephew had an exceptionally thin voice. I wondered if it was he who had been given Mr Dhameeja's attaché case.

'Are you,' he asked, 'the same Felu Mitter who solved the mystery of the Golden Fortress?'

'Yes,' said Feluda briefly, and leant back in his chair, crossing his legs, perfectly relaxed.

I kept looking at the other man. His face seemed familiar. Where had I seen him before? Then something seemed to jog my memory.

'Have you ever acted in a film?' I asked.

The man cleared his throat.

'Yes, in *The Ghost*. It's a thriller. I play the villain. But it hasn't yet been released.'

'Your name . . . ?'

'My real name is Prabeer Lahiri. But my screen name is Amar Kumar.'

'Oh yes, now I remember. I have seen your

photograph in a film magazine.'

Heavens, what kind of a villain would he make with a voice like that?

'Are you a professional actor?' asked Feluda. For some strange reason, Prabeer Babu was still standing.

'I have to help my uncle in his business,' he replied, 'which means going to his plastic factory. But my real interest is in acting.'

'What does your uncle think?'

'Uncle isn't . . . very enthusiastic about it.'

'Why not?'

'That's the way he is.'

Amar Kumar's face grew grave. Clearly, he had had arguments with his uncle over his career in films.

'I have to ask you something,' Feluda said politely, possibly because Amar Kumar was beginning to look belligerent.

'I don't mind answering your questions,' he said. 'What I can't stand is my uncle's constant digs at my—'

'Did your uncle recently give you an Air-India attaché case?'

'Yes, but someone pinched it. We've got a new servant, you see . . .'

Feluda raised a reassuring hand and smiled.

'No, no one stole that case, I assure you. It's with me.'

'With you?' Prabeer Babu seemed perfectly taken aback.

'Yes. Your uncle decided to return the case to its owner. He hired me for this purpose. What I want to know is whether you removed anything from it.'

'I did, naturally. Here it is.'

Prabeer Babu took out a ballpoint pen from his pocket. 'I wanted to use the blades and the shaving cream,' he added, 'but of course I never got the chance.'

'You do realize, don't you, that the case must go back to the owner with every item intact?'

'Yes, yes, naturally.'

He handed the pen over to Feluda. But he was obviously still greatly annoyed with his uncle. 'At least,' he muttered, 'I should have been told the case was going back. After all, he did give . . . '

He couldn't finish his sentence. Dinanath Babu's car sounded its horn at this moment, thereby causing the film villain to beat a quick retreat.

'Oh no, have you been waiting long?' Dinanath Babu walked into the room, looking slightly rueful, his hands folded in a namaskar. We stood up to greet him. 'No, no, please sit down,' he said hurriedly. 'You wouldn't mind a cup of tea, would you?'

His servant appeared almost immediately and left with an order to bring us tea. Dinanath Babu sat down on the settee next to ours.

'So . . . tell me . . . ?' he invited.

'Your case got exchanged with the man who gave you the apple. His name is G. C. Dhameeja.'

Dinanath Babu grew round-eyed. 'You found that out in just a day? What is this—magic?'

Feluda gave his famous lopsided smile and continued, 'He lives in Simla and I've got his address. He was supposed to spend three days at the Grand, but he left a day early.'

'Has he left already?' Dinanath Babu asked, a little regretfully.

'Yes. He left the hotel, but we don't know whether he returned to Simla. One telegram to his house in Simla, and you shall get an answer to that.'

Dinanath Babu seemed to ponder for a few moments. Then he said, 'All right. I will send a cable today. But if I discover he has indeed gone back to Simla, I still have to return his case to him, don't I?'

'Yes, of course. And yours has to come back to you. I am quite curious about that travelogue.'

'Very good. Allow me to make a proposal, Mr Mitter. Why don't you go to Simla with your cousin? I shall, of course, pay all your expenses. It's snowing in Simla, I hear. Have you ever seen it snow, Khoka?'

At any other time, I would have been affronted at being called a child. But now it did not seem to matter at all. Go to Simla? Oh, how exciting! My heart started to race faster.

But Feluda's next words were most annoying. 'You must think this one through, Mr Lahiri,' he said. 'It's just a matter of taking an attaché case to Simla, and bringing one back, isn't it? So anyone can do the job. It doesn't necessarily have to be me.'

'No, no, no,' Dinanath Babu protested rather vehemently, 'where will I find anyone as reliable as you? And since you began the investigation, I think you should end it.'

'Why, you have a nephew, don't you?'

A shadow passed over Dinanath Babu's face.

'He is no good, really. I'm afraid my nephew's sense of responsibility is virtually nonexistent. Do you know what he has done? He's gone into films! No, I cannot rely on him at all. I'd rather the two of you went. I'll tell my travel agents to make all arrangements. You can fly up to Delhi and then catch a train. When you've done your job, you can even have a holiday in Simla for a few days. It would give me a lot of pleasure to be of service to a man like you. What you've done in just a few hours is truly remarkable!'

The tea arrived, together with cakes and sandwiches. Feluda picked up a piece of chocolate cake and said, 'Thank you. There is one little thing I am still feeling curious about. The Nepali box in which you found the manuscript. Is it possible to see it?'

'Of course. That's not a problem at all. I'll get my bearer to bring it.'

The box appeared in a few moments. About two feet in length and ten inches in height, its wooden surface was covered by a sheet of copper. Red, blue and yellow stones were set on the lid. The smell that greeted my nostrils as soon as the lid was lifted was the same as that in Naresh Pakrashi's study. Dust-covered old furniture and threadbare curtains gave out the same musty smell.

Dinanath Babu said, 'As you can see, there are two compartments in the box. The manuscript was in the first one, wrapped in a Nepali newspaper.'

'Good heavens, it's stuffed with so many different things!' exclaimed Feluda.

'Yes,' Dinanath Babu smiled. 'You might call it a mini curio shop. But it's so filthy I haven't felt tempted to handle anything.'

It turned out that the compartments could be removed. Feluda brought out the second one and inspected the objects it contained. There were stone necklaces, little engraved discs made of copper and brass, two candles, a small bell, a couple of little bowls, a bone of some unknown animal, a few dried herbs and flowers, reduced to dust—truly a little junk shop.

'Did this box belong to your uncle?'

'It came with him, so I assume it did.'

'When did he return from Kathmandu?'

'In 1923. He died the same year. I was seven.'

'Very interesting,' said Feluda. Then he took a last sip from his cup and stood up. 'I accept your proposal, Mr Lahiri,' he said, 'but we cannot leave tomorrow. We'll have to collect our warm clothes from the dry-cleaner's. The day after tomorrow might be a better idea. And please don't forget to cable Dhameeja.'

We returned home at around half-past-eight to find Jatayu waiting for us in the living-room, a brown parcel on his lap.

'Have you been to the pictures?' he asked with a smile.

Chapter 4

Jatayu was the pseudonym of Lalmohan Ganguli, the famous writer of best-selling crime thrillers. We had first met him on our way to the golden fortress in Rajasthan. There are some men who appear strangely comical without any apparent reason. Lalmohan Babu was one of them. He was short—the top of his head barely reached Feluda's shoulder; he wore size five shoes, was painfully thin, and yet would occasionally fold one of his arms absentmindedly and feel his biceps with the other. The next instant, he would give a violent start if anyone so much as sneezed loudly in the next room.

'I brought my latest book for you and Tapesh,' he said, offering the brown parcel to Feluda. He had started coming to our house fairly regularly ever since our adventure in Rajasthan.

'Which country did you choose this time?' Feluda asked, unwrapping the parcel. The spine-chilling escapades of Lalmohan Babu's hero involved moving through different countries.

'Oh, I have covered practically the whole world this time,' Lalmohan Babu replied proudly, 'from the Nilgiris to the North Pole.'

'I hope there are no factual errors this time?' Feluda said quizzically, passing the book to me. Feluda had had to correct a mistake in his last book, *The Sahara Shivers*, regarding a camel's water supply.

'No, sir,' Lalmohan Babu grinned. 'One of my neighbours has a full set of the *Encyclopaedia Britannia*. I checked every detail.'

'I'd have felt more reassured, Lalmohan Babu, if you had consulted the *Britannica* rather than the *Britannia*.'

But Jatayu ignored this remark and went on, 'The climax comes—you've got to read it—with my hero, Prakhar Rudra, having a fight with a hippopotamus.'

'A hippo?'

'Yes, it's really a thrilling affair.'

'Where does this fight take place?'

'Why, in the North Pole, of course. A hippo, didn't I say?'

'A hippopotamus in the North Pole?'

'Yes, yes. Haven't you seen pictures of this animal? It has whiskers like the bristles of a garden broom, fangs that stick out like a pair of white radishes, it pads softly on the snow . . .'

'That's a walrus, surely? A hippopotamus lives in Africa!'

Jatayu turned a deep shade of pink and bit his lip in profound embarrassment. 'Eh heh heh heh!' he said. 'Bad mistake, that! Tell you what, from now on I'll show you my manuscript before giving it to the publisher.'

Feluda made no reply to this. 'Excuse me,' he said and disappeared into his room.

'Your cousin appears a little quiet,' Lalmohan Babu said to me. 'Has he got a new case?'

'No, it's nothing important,' I told him. 'But we have to go to Simla in the next couple of days.'

'A long tour?'

'No, just about four days.'

'Hmm . . . I've never been to that part of the country . . . ' Lalmohan Babu grew preoccupied. But he began to show signs of animation the minute Feluda returned.

'Tapesh tells me you're going to Simla. Is it something to do with an investigation?'

'No, not exactly. It's just that Tom's case has got exchanged with Dick's. So we have to return Dick's case to him and collect Tom's.'

'Good lord, the mystery of the missing case? Or, simply, a mysterious case?'

'Look, I have no idea if there is any real mystery involved. But one or two things make me wonder . . . just a little . . . '

'Felu Babu,' Jatayu interrupted, 'I have come to know you pretty well in these few months. I'm convinced you wouldn't have taken the case unless you felt there was . . . well, something in it. Do tell me what it is.'

I could sense Feluda was reluctant to reveal too much at this stage. 'It's difficult to say anything,' he said guardedly, 'without knowing for sure who is telling lies, and who is telling the truth, or who is simply trying to conceal the truth. All I know is that there is something wrong somewhere.'

'All right, that's enough!' Jatayu's eyes began to shine. 'Just say the word, and I'll tag along with you.'

'Can you bear the cold?'

'Cold? I went to Darjeeling last year.'

'When?'

'In May.'

'It's snowing in Simla now.'

'What!' Lalmohan Babu rose from his chair in excitement. 'Sn-ow? You don't say! It was the desert the last time and now it's going to be snow? From the frying pan into the frigidaire? Oh, I can't imagine it!'

'It's going to be an expensive business.'

I knew Feluda was trying gently to discourage him, but Jatayu paid no attention to his words.

'I am not afraid of expenses,' he retorted, laughing like a film villain. 'I have published twenty-one thrillers, each one of which has seen at least five editions. I have bought three houses in Calcutta, by the grace of God. It's in my own interest that I travel as much as possible. The more places I see, the easier it is to think up new plots. And not everyone is clever like you, so most people can't see the difference between a walrus and a hippo, anyway. They'll happily swallow what I dish out, and that simply means that the cash keeps rolling in. Oh no, I am not bothered about the expenses. But if you give me a straight "no",' then obviously it's a different matter.'

Feluda gave in. Before taking his leave, Jatayu took

the details of when and how we'd be leaving and for how long, jotted these down in his notebook and said, 'Woollen vests, a couple of pullovers, a woollen jacket and an overcoat . . . surely that should be enough even for Simla?'

'Yes,' said Feluda gravely, 'but only if you add to it a pair of gloves, a Balaclava helmet, a pair of galoshes, woollen socks and something to fight frostbite. Then you may relax.'

I hate exams and tests in school, but I love the kind of tests Feluda sets for me. These are fun and they help clear my mind.

Feluda told me to come to his room after dinner. There he lay on his bed, flat on his stomach, and began throwing questions at me. The first was, 'Name all the people we've got to know who are related to this case.'

'Dinanath Lahiri.'

'OK. What sort of a man do you think he is?'

'All right, I guess. But he doesn't know much about books and writers. And I'm slightly doubtful about the way he is spending such a lot of money to send us to Simla.'

'A man who can maintain a couple of cars like that doesn't have to worry about money. Besides, you mustn't forget that employing Felu Mitter is a matter of prestige.'

'Well, in that case there is nothing to be doubtful about. The second person we met was Naresh Chandra Pakrashi. Very ill-tempered.'

'But plain spoken. That's good. Not many have that

quality.'

'But does he always tell the truth? I mean, how do we know that Dinanath Lahiri really used to go to the races?'

'Perhaps he still does. But that doesn't necessarily mean that he's a crook.'

'Then we met Prabeer Lahiri, alias Amar Kumar. Didn't seem to like his uncle.'

'That's perfectly natural. His uncle is a stumbling block in his way forward in films, he gives him an attaché case full of things one day, and then takes it back without telling him . . . so obviously he's annoyed with his uncle.'

'Prabeer Babu seemed pretty well built.'

'Yes, he has strong and broad wrists. Perhaps that's why his voice sounds so odd. It doesn't match his manly figure at all. Now tell me the names of the other passengers who travelled with Dinanath Lahiri.'

'One of them was Brijmohan. And his surname was . . . let me see . . . '

'Kedia. Marwari.'

'Yes. He's a moneylender. Nothing remarkable in his appearance, apparently. Knew Mr Pakrashi.'

'He really does have an office in Lenin Sarani. I looked it up in the telephone directory.'

'I see. Well, the other was G. C. Dhameeja. He lives in Simla. Has an orchard.'

'So he said. We don't know that for sure.'

'But it is his attaché case that got exchanged with Mr Lahiri's. Surely there is no doubt about that?'

The case in question was lying open next to Feluda's bed. He stared absentmindedly at its contents and muttered, 'Hmm . . . yes, that is perhaps the only thing one can be . . . ' He broke off and picked up the two English newspapers that were in the case and glanced at them. 'These,' he continued to mutter, 'are the only things that . . . you know . . . make me feel doubtful. They don't fit in somehow.'

At this point, he had to stop muttering for the phone rang. Feluda had had an extension put in his own room.

'Hello.'

'Is that you, Mr Mitter?'

I could hear the words spoken from the other side, possibly because it was quiet outside.

'Yes, Mr Lahiri.'

'Listen, I have just received a message from Dhameeja.'

'You mean he's replied to your telegram? Already?'

'No, no. I don't think I'll get a reply before tomorrow. I am talking about a phone call. Apparently, Dhameeja had gone to the railway reservation office and got my name and address from them. But because he had to leave very suddenly, he could not contact me himself. He left my attaché case with a friend here in Calcutta. It was this friend who rang me. He'll return my case to me if I bring Dhameeja's. So, you see . . . '

'Did you ask him if the manuscript was still there?'

'Oh yes. Everything's fine.'

'That's good news then. Your problem's solved.'

'Yes, most unexpectedly. I'm leaving in five minutes. I'll collect Dhameeja's case from you and then go to Pretoria Street.'

'May I make a request?'

'Certainly.'

'Why should you take the trouble of going out? We were going to go all the way to Simla, weren't we? So we'd quite happily go to Pretoria Street and collect your case for you. If you let me keep it tonight, I can skim through Shambhucharan's tale of Tibet. You may treat that as my fee. Tomorrow morning I shall return both the case and the manuscript to you.'

'Very well. I have no objection to that at all. The man who rang me is a Mr Puri and his address is 4/2 Pretoria Street.'

'Thank you. All's well that ends well.'

Feluda replaced the receiver and sat frowning. I, too, sat silently, fighting a wave of disappointment. I did so want to go to Simla and see it snow. Now I had missed the chance and would have to rot in Calcutta where it was already uncomfortably hot, even in March. Well, I suppose I ought to be with Feluda in this last chapter of the story.

'Let me go and get changed, Feluda,' I said. 'I won't be a minute.'

'All right. Hurry up.'

Twenty minutes later, we were in a taxi, cruising up and down Pretoria Street. It was a quiet street and, it being nearly half past eleven at night, not a soul was to be seen. We drove from one end of the street to the other, but it was impossible to see the numbers on the houses from the car. 'Please wait here, Sardarji,' Feluda said to the driver. 'We'll find the house and come back. We simply have to drop this case. It won't take long.'

An amiable man, the driver agreed to wait. We got out of the taxi at one end of the road and began walking. Beyond the wall on our left stood the tall and silent

Birla building, dwarfing every other building in its vicinity with all its twenty-two floors. I had often heard Feluda remark that the creepiest things in a city after nightfall were its skyscrapers. 'Have you ever seen a corpse standing up?' he had asked me once. 'These buildings are just that in the dark—just a body without life or soul!'

A few minutes later, we found a house with '4' written on its gate. The next house, which was at some distance, turned out to be number 5. So 4/2 was probably in the little lane that ran between numbers 4 and 5. It was very difficult to see anything clearly. The few dim streetlights did nothing to help. We stepped into the lane, walking cautiously. How quiet it was!

Here was another gate. This must be 4/1. Where was 4/2? Somewhere further down, hidden in the dark? There didn't seem to be another house in the lane and, even if there was, it certainly did not have a light on. There were walls on both sides of the lane. Overgrown branches of trees on the other side hung over these. A very faint noise of traffic came from the main road. A clock struck in the distance. It must be the clock in St Paul's Church. It was now exactly half past eleven. But these noises did nothing to improve the eerie silence in Pretoria Street. A dog barked nearby. And, in that instant—

'Taxi! Sardarji, Sardarji!' I screamed, quite involuntarily.

A man had jumped over the wall on our right and fallen over Feluda. He was followed by another. The attaché case Feluda was carrying was no longer in his hand. He had dropped it on the ground and was trying to tackle the first man. I could feel the two men struggling with each other, but could see nothing. The blue case was lying on the road, right in front of me. I stretched my hand to pick it up, but the second man turned around at this moment and knocked me aside. Then he snatched the case and rushed to the entrance of the lane, through which we had just stepped. On my left, Feluda and the other man were still grappling with each other, but I could not figure out what the problem was. Feluda, by this time, should have been able to overpower his opponent.

'God!'

This exclamation came from our driver. He had heard me scream and rushed out to help. But the man who was making off with the case knocked him down and vanished. I could see the poor driver lying flat on the ground under a streetlight. In the meantime, the first man managed to wriggle free from Feluda's grasp and climbed over the wall.

Feluda took out his handkerchief and began wiping his hands.

'That man,' he observed, 'had oiled himself rather well. Must have rubbed at least a kilo of mustard oil on his body, making him slippery as an eel. I believe it's an old trick with thieves.'

True. I had smelt the oil as soon as the two men arrived, but had not been able to guess where it was coming from.

'Thank God!'

For the life of me, I could not understand why Feluda said this. How could he, even after such a disaster? 'What do you mean?' I asked, puzzled. Feluda did not reply at once. He helped the driver, who appeared unhurt, to his feet. Then he said, as the three of us began walking towards the taxi, 'You don't think what those scoundrels got away with was Dhameeja's property, do you?'

'Wasn't it?' I was even more mystified.

'What they took was the property of Pradosh C. Mitter. And what it contained were three torn vests, five threadbare handkerchiefs, several pieces of rag and a few old newspapers, torn to shreds. I rang telephone enquiries when you went to change. They told me there was no telephone at 4/2 Pretoria Street. But, of course, I didn't know that even the address was a fake one.'

My heart started pounding once more. Something told me the visit to Simla was now imperative.

CHAPTER 5

We rang Dinanath Babu as soon as we got home. He was completely nonplussed. 'Goodness me!' he exclaimed, 'I had no idea a thing like this could happen! One possible explanation is, of course, that those two men were just ordinary thieves without any particular motive to steal Dhameeja's attaché case. But even so, the fact remains that both this man called Puri and the address he gave, were totally fictitious. That means Mr Dhameeja never really went to the railway reservation office. Who, then, made the phone call?'

'If we knew that, there would be no need for further investigations, Mr Lahiri.'

'But tell me, what made you suspicious in the first place?'

'The fact that the man rang you so late in the night. Mr Dhameeja went back yesterday. So why didn't Mr

Puri give you a call yesterday or during the day today?'

'I see. Well, it looks as though we have to go back to our original plan of sending you to Simla. But considering the turn this whole business is taking, frankly I am now scared to send you anywhere.'

Feluda laughed, 'Don't worry, Mr Lahiri. I can't call your case tame and insipid any more. It's definitely got a taste of excitement. And I am glad, for I would have felt ashamed to take your money otherwise. Anyway, I would now like you to do something for me, please.'

'Yes?'

'Let me have a list of the contents of your case. It would make it easier for me to check when Dhameeja returns it.'

'That's easy since there wasn't anything much, anyway. But I'll let you have the list when I send you your tickets.'

Feluda left home early the next morning. His whole demeanour had changed in just a few hours. I could tell by the way he kept cracking his knuckles that he was feeling restless and disturbed. Like me, he had not been able to work out why anyone should try to steal a case that contained nothing of value. He had examined each item carefully once more, going so far as squeezing some of the toothpaste out and feeling the shaving cream by pressing the tube gently. He even took out the blades from their container and unfolded the newspapers. Still, he found nothing suspicious. Feluda left at about 8 a.m. 'I will return at eleven,' he said before leaving. 'If anyone rings the calling bell in the next three hours, don't open the door yourself. Get Srinath to do it.'

I resigned myself to wait patiently for his return. Baba had gone out of town. So I wrote a letter for him, explaining why Feluda and I had to go to Simla before he got back. Having done this, I settled down on the settee in the living-room with a book. But I could not read. The more I thought about Feluda's new case, the more confused I felt. Dinanath Babu, his nephew who acted in films, the irascible Mr Pakrashi, Mr Dhameeja of Simla, the moneylender called Brijmohan . . . everyone seemed unreal, as though each was wearing a mask. Even the contents of the Air-India case seemed false. And, on top of everything else, was last night's frightening experience . . .

No, I must stop thinking. I picked up a magazine. It was a film magazine called *Sparkling Stars*. Ah yes, here was the photograph of Amar Kumar I had seen before. 'The newcomer, Amar Kumar, in the latest film being made by Sri Guru Pictures', said the caption. Amar Kumar was staring straight into the camera, wearing a cap very much in the style of Dev Anand in *Jewel Thief*, a scarf around his throat, a cruel smile under a pencil-thin moustache. There was a pistol in his hand, very obviously a fake, possibly made of wood.

Something made me suddenly jump up and turn to the telephone directory. Here it was—Sri Guru Pictures, 53 Bentinck Street. 24554.

I dialled the number quickly. It rang several times before someone answered at the other end.

'Hello.'

'Is that Sri Guru Pictures?'

My voice had recently started to break. So I was sure whoever I was speaking to would never guess I was really no more than fifteen-and-a-half.

'Yes, this is Sri Guru Pictures.'

'This is about Amar Kumar, you know . . . the newcomer in your latest film—'

'Please speak to Mr Mallik.' The telephone was passed to another man.

'Yes?'

'Mr Mallik?'

'Speaking.'

'Is there someone called Amar Kumar working in your latest film? *The Ghost*, I think it's called?'

'Amar Kumar has been dropped.'

'Dropped?'

'Who am I speaking to, please?'

'I . . . well, I . . . '

Like a fool, I could think of nothing to say and put the receiver down hurriedly.

So Amar Kumar was no longer in the cast! It must have been because of his voice. How unfair, though, to reject him after his picture had been published in a magazine. But didn't the man know, or did he simply pretend to us that he was still acting in the film?

I was lost in thought when the telephone rang, startling me considerably.

'Hello!' I gasped.

There was no response for a few seconds. Then I heard a faint click. Oh, I knew. Someone was calling from a public pay phone.

'Hello?' I said again. This time, I heard a voice, soft but distinct.

'Going to Simla, are you?'

This was the last thing I'd have expected to hear from a strange voice. Rendered speechless, I could only swallow in silence.

The voice spoke again. It sounded harsh and the words it uttered chilled my blood. 'Danger. Do you hear? You are both going to be in great danger if you go to Simla.' This was followed by another click. The line was disconnected. But I didn't need to hear any more. Those few words were enough. Like the Nepali Rana in Uncle Sidhu's story, whose hand shook while shooting at a tiger, I replaced the receiver with a trembling hand.

Then I flopped down on a chair and sat very still. About half an hour later, I heard another ring. This nearly made me fall off the chair, but this time I realized it was the door bell, not the telephone. It was past eleven, so I opened the door myself and Feluda walked in. The huge packets in his hands meant that he had been to the laundry to collect our warm clothes.

Feluda gave me a sidelong glance and said, 'Why are you licking your lips? Has there been a strange phone call?'

'How did you guess?' I asked, astonished.

'From the way you've kept the receiver. Besides, the whole thing's become so complicated that I'd have been surprised if we didn't get a few weird calls. Who was it? What did he say?'

'Don't know who it was. He said going to Simla meant danger for both of us.'

Feluda pushed the regulator of the fan to its maximum speed and sat casually down on the divan.

'What did you say to him?'

'Nothing.'

'Idiot! You should have said going to Simla cannot possibly be more dangerous than going out in the street in Calcutta. A regular battlefield is probably the only place that can claim to be more full of danger than the streets in this city.'

Feluda's nonchalance calmed my nerves. I decided to change the subject.

'Where did you go?' I asked. 'Apart from the laundry, I mean.'

'To the office of S. M. Kedia.'

'Did you learn anything new?'

'Brijmohan seemed a friendly enough fellow. His family has lived in Calcutta for three generations. And yes, he knows Mr Pakrashi. I got the impression that Pakrashi still owes him some money. Brijmohan, too, had eaten the apple Dhameeja had offered him. But no, he doesn't have a blue Air-India attaché case; and he had spent most of his time on the train either sleeping or just lying with his eyes closed.'

I told Feluda about Amar Kumar.

'If he knows he has been dropped but is pretending he isn't,' remarked Feluda, 'then the man is truly a fine actor.'

We finished our packing in the late afternoon. Since we were going for less than a week, I didn't take too many clothes. At six-thirty in the evening, Jatayu rang us.

'I am taking a new weapon,' he informed us. 'I'll show it to you when we get to Delhi.'

We knew he was interested in collecting weapons

of various kind. He had taken a Nepali dagger on our journey through Rajasthan, although he did not get the chance to use it.

'I have bought my ticket,' he added. 'I'll see you tomorrow at the airport.'

Our tickets arrived a couple of hours later, together with a note from Dinanath Babu. It said:

Dear Mr Mitter,
I am enclosing your air tickets to Delhi and train tickets to Simla. I have made reservations for you for a day in Delhi at the Janpath Hotel; and you are booked at the Clarkes in Simla for four days. I have just received a reply from Mr Dhameeja. He says he has my attaché case safe. He expects you to call on him the day after tomorrow at 4 p.m. You have got his address, so I will not repeat it here. I have not made a list of the items in my case because, thinking things over, it struck me that there is only one thing in it that is of any value to me. It is a bottle of enterovioform tablets. These are made in England and definitely more effective than those produced here. I should be happy simply to get these back. I hope you have a safe and successful visit.
Yours sincerely,
Dinanath Lahiri

We were planning to have an early night and go to bed by ten o' clock, but at a quarter to ten, the door bell rang. Who could it be at this hour? I opened the door and was immediately struck dumb to find a man who I never dreamt would ever pay us a visit. If Feluda was similarly surprised, he did not show it.

'Good evening, Mr Pakrashi,' he said coolly, 'please come in.'

Mr Pakrashi came in, a slightly embarrassed look on his face, a smile hovering on his lips. His ill-tempered air was gone. What had happened in a day to bring about this miraculous change? And what had he come to tell us so late in the evening?

He sat down on a chair and said, 'Sorry to trouble you. I know it's late. I did try to ring you, but couldn't get through. So I thought it was best to call personally. Please don't mind.'

'We don't. Do tell us what brings you here.'

'I have come to make a request. It is a very special request. In fact, it may strike you as positively strange.'

'Really?'

'You said something about a manuscript in Dinanath Lahiri's attaché case. Was it . . . something written by Shambhucharan Bose? You know, the same man who wrote about the Terai?'

'Yes, indeed. An account of his visit to Tibet.'

'My God!'

Feluda did not say anything. Naresh Pakrashi, too, was quiet for a few moments. Then he said, 'Are you aware that my collection of travelogues is the largest and the best in Calcutta?'

'I am fully prepared to believe that. I did happen to glance at those almirahs in your room; and I caught the names of quite a few very well-known travel writers.'

'Your powers of observation must be very good.'

'That is what I live by, Mr Pakrashi.'

Mr Pakrashi now took the pipe out of his mouth, looked straight at Feluda and said, 'You are going to Simla, aren't you?'

It was Feluda's turn to be surprised. He did not actually ask, 'How do you know?' But his eyes held a quizzical look.

Mr Pakrashi smiled. 'A clever man like you,' he said, 'would naturally not find it too difficult to discover that Dinu Lahiri's attaché case had got exchanged with Dhameeja's. I had seen Dhameeja's name written on his suitcase. He did, in fact, take out his shaving things from the blue Air-India case, so I knew it was his.'

'Why didn't you say so yesterday?'

'Isn't it a greater joy to have worked things out for yourself? It is your case, after all. You will work on it and get paid for your pains. Why should I voluntarily offer any help?'

Feluda appeared to be in agreement. All he said was, 'But you haven't yet told me what your strange request is.'

'I am coming to that. You will—no doubt—manage to retrieve Dinanath's case. And the manuscript with it. I would request you not to give it back to him.'

'What!' This time Feluda could not conceal his surprise. Nor could I.

'I suggest you pass the manuscript to me.'

'To you?' Feluda raised his voice.

'I told you it would sound odd. But you must listen to me,' Mr Pakrashi continued, leaning forward a little, his elbows resting on his knees. 'Dinanath Lahiri cannot appreciate the value of that book. Did you see a single good book in his house? No, I know you did not. Besides, don't think I'm not going to compensate you for this. I have got—'

Here he stopped and took out a long blue envelope from the inside pocket of his jacket. Then he opened it and offered it to Feluda. It was stuffed with new, crisp, sweet-smelling hundred-rupee notes. 'I have two thousand here,' he said, 'and this is only an advance payment. I will give you another two thousand when you hand over the manuscript to me.'

Feluda did not even glance at the envelope. He took out a cigarette from his pocket, lit it casually and said, 'I don't think it's of any relevance whether Dinanath Lahiri appreciates the value of the manuscript or not. I have promised to collect his case from Dhameeja in Simla and return it to him, with all its contents intact. And that is what I am going to do.'

Mr Pakrashi appeared to be at a loss to find a suitable answer to this. After a few moments, he simply said, 'All right. Let's forget about your payment. All I am asking you to do is give me the manuscript. Tell Lahiri it was missing. Say Dhameeja said he didn't see it.'

'How,' asked Feluda, 'can I put Mr Dhameeja in a position like that? Can you think of the consequences? You can't seriously expect me to tell lies about a totally innocent man? No, Mr Pakrashi, I cannot do as you ask.'

Feluda rose and added, perfectly civilly, 'Goodnight, Mr Pakrashi. I hope you will not misunderstand me.'

Mr Pakrashi continued to sit, staring into space.

Then he replaced the envelope into his pocket, stood up, gave Feluda a dry smile and went out without a word. It was impossible to tell from his face whether he felt angry, disappointed or humiliated.

Would any other sleuth have been able to resist such temptation and behave the way Feluda had done? Perhaps not.

CHAPTER 6

Feluda, Jatayu and I were sitting in Indian Airlines flight number 263, on our way to Delhi. The plane left at 7.30 a.m. Feluda had explained to Jatayu, while we were waiting in the departure lounge, about our visit to Pretoria Street and the ensuing events. Jatayu listened, round-eyed, occasionally breaking into exclamations like 'thrilling!' and 'highly suspicious!' Then he jotted down in his notebook the little matter of the thief and the mustard oil.

'Have you flown before?' I asked him.

'If,' he replied sagely, 'a man's imagination is lively enough, he can savour an experience without actually doing anything. No, I've never travelled by air. But if you asked me whether I'm feeling nervous, my answer would be "not a bit" because in my imagination, I have travelled not just in an aeroplane but also in a rocket.

Yes, I have been to the moon!'

Despite these brave words, when the plane began to speed across the runway just before take-off, I saw Lalmohan Babu clutching the armrests of his seat so tightly that his knuckles turned white. When the plane actually shot up in the air, his colour turned a rather unhealthy shade of yellow and his face broke into a terrible grimace.

'What happened to you?' I asked him afterwards.

'But that was natural!' he said. 'When a rocket leaves for outer space, even the faces of astronauts get distorted. The thing is, you see, as you're leaving the ground, the laws of gravity pull you back. In that conflict, the facial muscles contract, and hence the distortion of the whole face.'

I wanted to ask if that was indeed the case, why should Lalmohan Babu be the only person to be singled out by the laws of gravity, why didn't everyone else get similarly affected; but seeing that he had recovered his composure and was, in fact, looking quite cheerful, I said nothing more.

Breakfast arrived soon, with the cutlery wrapped in a cellophane sheet. Lalmohan Babu attacked his omelette with the coffee spoon, used the knife like a spoon to scoop out the marmalade from its little pot, putting it straight into his mouth without bothering to spread it on a piece of bread; then he tried to peel the orange with his fork, but gave up soon and used his fingers instead.

Finally, he leant forward and said to Feluda, 'I saw you chewing betel-nut a while ago. Do you have any left?'

Feluda took out the Kodak container from the blue attaché case and passed it to Lalmohan Babu. I couldn't help glancing again at Mr Dhameeja's case. Did it know that we were going to travel twelve hundred miles to a snow-laden place situated at a height of seven thousand feet, simply to return it to its owner and pick up an identical one? The thought suddenly made me shiver.

Feluda had said virtually nothing after we took off. He had taken out his famous blue notebook (volume seven) and was scribbling in it, occasionally looking up to stare out of the window at the fluffy white clouds, biting the end of his pen. It was impossible to tell what he was thinking. I, for my part, had given up trying to think at all. It was all too complex.

We soon landed in Delhi and came out of the airport. There was a noticeable nip in the air. 'This probably means there has been a fresh snowfall in Simla,' Feluda observed. He was still clutching the blue case. Not for a second had he allowed himself to be separated from it.

'I think I can get a room at the Agra Hotel,' said Lalmohan Babu. 'I will join you at the Janpath by noon. Then we can have lunch together and have a little roam around. The train to Simla doesn't leave until eight this evening, does it?'

The Janpath was a fairly large hotel. We were given room 532 on the fifth floor. Feluda put our luggage on the luggage-rack and threw himself on the bed. I decided to take this opportunity to ask him something that I had been feeling curious about.

'Feluda,' I said, 'in this whole business of blue cases and jumping hooligans, what strikes you as most suspicious?'

'The newspapers.'

'Er . . . would you care to elaborate?' I asked hesitantly.

'I cannot figure out why Mr Dhameeja folded the two newspapers so neatly and put them in his case with such care. A newspaper, once read, especially on a train, is useless. Most people would leave it behind without a second thought. Then why . . . ?'

This was Feluda's technique. He would begin to worry about a seemingly completely irrelevant point that would escape everyone else. Certainly I couldn't make head or tail of it.

In the remaining hours that we spent in Delhi, two things happened. The first was nothing remarkable, but the other was horrifying.

Lalmohan Babu turned up at about half past twelve. We decided to go to the Jantar Mantar, which was not far from our hotel. Jatayu and I were both keen to see this observatory built two hundred and fifty years ago by Sawai Jai Singh. Feluda said he'd much rather stay in the hotel, both to keep an eye on Dhameeja's attaché case and to think more about the mystery.

The first incident took place within ten minutes of our arrival at the Jantar Mantar. We were strolling along peacefully, when suddenly Lalmohan Babu clutched at my sleeve and whispered, 'I think . . . I think a rather suspicious character is trying to follow us!'

I looked at the man he indicated. It was an old man, a Nepali cap on his head, cotton wool plugged in his ears, his eyes hidden behind a pair of dark glasses. It did appear as though he was interested in our movements. How very strange!

'I know that man!' said Jatayu.

'What!'

'He sat next to me on the plane. Helped me fasten my seat belt.'

'Did he speak to you?'

'No. I thanked him, but he said nothing. Most suspicious, I tell you!'

Perhaps the man could guess we were talking about him. He disappeared only a few minutes later.

By the time we returned to the hotel, it was almost half past three. I asked for our key at the reception, but the receptionist said he didn't have it. This alarmed me somewhat, but then I remembered I had not handed it in at all. It was still in my pocket. Besides, it was rather foolish to worry about the key when Feluda was in the room to let us in. 'Just goes to show you're not used to staying in hotels,' I told myself.

Our room was on the right, about thirty yards down the corridor. I knocked on the door. There was no response.

'Perhaps your cousin is having a nap,' remarked Lalmohan Babu.

I knocked again. Nothing happened.

Then I turned the handle and discovered that the door was open. But I knew Feluda had locked it from inside when we left.

I pushed the door, but it refused to open more than a little. Something pretty heavy must be lying behind it. What could it be?

I peered in through the little gap, and my blood froze.

Feluda was lying on the floor, face down. His right elbow was what the door was knocking against.

I could hardly breathe, but knew that I must not panic. Together with Lalmohan Babu, I pushed the door harder and eventually we both managed to slide in.

Feluda was unconscious. But, possibly as a result of our pushing and heaving, he was beginning to stir and groan. Lalmohan Babu, it turned out, could keep a calm head in a crisis. It was he who splashed cold water on Feluda's face and fanned him furiously until he opened his eyes.

Then he raised a hand gingerly and felt the centre of his head, making a face. 'It's gone, I assume?' he asked. I had already checked.

'Yes, Feluda,' I had to tell him, 'that attaché case has vanished.'

Feluda staggered to his feet, declining our offer of assistance.

'It's all right,' he insisted, 'I can manage. I've got a bump on my head, but I think that's all. It might have been worse.'

It might indeed. Feluda took a few minutes to rest and to make sure nothing was broken. Then he rang room service, ordered tea for us all and told us what had happened.

'I studied the entries in my notebook for about half an hour after you had gone. Then I began to feel tired. I hadn't slept for more than a couple of hours last night, you see. So I thought I'd have a little rest, but just at that moment the telephone rang.'

'The telephone? Who was it?'

'Wait, let me finish. It was the receptionist. He said,

"Mr Mitter, there's a gentleman here who has recognized you. He says he'd like to take the autograph of such a brilliant sleuth as yourself. Shall I send him up?"'

Feluda paused here, turned to me and continued, 'I realized one thing today, Topshe, and I don't mind admitting it—to give an autograph is as tempting as taking it. I shall, of course, be more careful in future. But I needed this lesson.'

'What does that mean?'

'I felt so pleased that I told the receptionist to send the man up. He came, knocked on the door, I opened it, felt a sharp knock on my own head, and . . . everything went black. The man had covered his face with a large handkerchief, so I don't even know what he looked like.'

'Since we are in Delhi,' suggested Jatayu, 'wouldn't it be a good idea to inform the Prime Minister?'

Feluda smiled wryly at this. 'God knows what that man gained by stealing that blue case,' he remarked, 'but he has certainly put us in an impossible situation. What a reckless devil!'

For the next few minutes, no one spoke. All that could be heard in the room was the sound of sighs. At last, Feluda uttered a few significant words. 'There is a way,' he said slowly. 'Not, I admit, a simple way. But it's the only one I can think of, and we've got to take it because we cannot go to Simla empty-handed.'

He reached for his blue notebook, and ran his eyes through the list of contents in Dhameeja's case.

'There is nothing in this list,' he said, 'that we can't get here in Delhi. We've got to get every item. I remember what each one looked like and what condition it was in. So that's one thing we needn't worry about. I could make the toothpaste and the shaving cream look old and used. And it should be possible to get hold of a white handkerchief and have it embroidered. I remember the pattern. The newspapers will, of course, have a different date, but I don't think Mr Dhameeja will notice it. The only expensive thing would be a roll of Kodak film . . .'

'Hey!' Lalmohan Babu interrupted. 'Hey, look, I completely forgot to give this back to you. You passed it to me on the plane, remember?' He returned the Kodak container to Feluda.

'Good, that's one problem solved . . . but what is that sticking out of your pocket?'

A piece of paper had slipped out with the little box of betel-nuts. We could all see what was written on it:

'Do not go to Simla if you value your life.'

CHAPTER 7

It was now 9.30 p.m. Our train was rushing through the darkness in the direction of Kalka. We would have to change at Kalka to go on to Simla. There were only the three of us in our compartment. The fourth berth was empty. I couldn't guess how the other two were feeling, but in my own mind there was a mixture of so many different emotions that it was impossible to tell which was the uppermost: excitement, pleasure, an eager anticipation or fear.

Lalmohan Babu broke the silence by saying, somewhat hesitantly, 'Tell me, Mr Mitter, the dividing line between a brilliant detective and a criminal with real cunning is really quite thin, isn't it?'

Feluda was so preoccupied that he did not reply. But I knew very well what had prompted the question. It was related to a certain incident that took place during the evening. I should describe it in some detail, for it revealed a rather unexpected streak in Feluda's character.

It had taken us barely half an hour to collect most of the things we needed to deceive Mr Dhameeja. The only major problem was the attaché case itself.

Where could we find a blue Air-India case? We didn't know anyone in Delhi we could ask. It might be possible to get a similar blue case in a shop—but that wouldn't have Air-India written on it. And that would, naturally, give the whole show away.

In the end, however, in sheer desperation, we did buy a plain blue case and, clutching it in one hand, Feluda led us into the main office of Air-India.

The first person our eyes fell on was an old man, a Parsee cap on his head, sitting right next to the 'Enquiries' counter. On his left, resting against his chair, was a brand new blue Air-India attaché case, exactly the kind we were looking for.

Feluda walked straight up to the counter and placed his own case beside the old man's. 'Is there an Air-India flight to Frankfurt from Delhi?' he asked the man behind the counter. In a matter of seconds, he got the necessary information, said, 'Thank you,' picked up the old man's case and pushed his own to the spot where it had been resting and coolly walked out. Lalmohan Babu and I followed, quite speechless. Then we returned to the hotel and Feluda began to work on the attaché case. By the time he finished, no one—not even Mr Dhameeja—could have said that it was not the one we had been given by Dinanath Lahiri. The same applied to its contents.

Feluda had been staring at his notebook. Now he shut it, rose and began pacing. 'It was just like this,' he muttered. 'Those four men were in a coach exactly like this . . .'

I have always found it difficult to tell what would attract Feluda's attention. Right now, he was staring at the glasses that stood inside metal rings attached to the wall. Why should these be of any interest to him?

'Can you sleep in a moving train, or can't you?' he asked Lalmohan Babu, rather abruptly.

'Well, I . . .' Lalmohan Babu replied, trying to suppress a giant yawn, 'I quite like being rocked.'

'Yes. I know the rocking generally helps one sleep. But not everyone, mind you. I have an uncle who cannot sleep a wink in a train,' said Feluda and jumped up on the empty berth. Then he switched on the reading lamp, opened the book that was in Dhameeja's attaché case, and turned a few pages. We had bought a second copy at a book stall in the New Delhi railway station.

Laying the book aside, Feluda stretched on the upper berth and stared up at the ceiling. It was completely dark outside. Nothing could be seen except a few flickering lights in the distance.

I was about to ask Lalmohan Babu if he had remembered to bring his weapon and, if so, when would he show it to us, when he spoke unexpectedly.

'We forgot one thing,' he said, 'betel-nuts. We must check with the fellow from the dining car if they have any. If not, we shall have to buy some at the next station. There's just one left in this little box.'

Lalmohan Babu took out the Kodak container, the only original object left from Dhameeja's attaché case, and tilted it on his palm. The betel-nut did not slip out.

'How annoying!' he exclaimed. 'I can see it, but it won't come out!' He began to shake the container vigorously, showering strong words on the obstinate piece of betel-nut, but it refused to budge.

'Give it to me!' said Feluda and leapt down from the upper berth, snatching the container from Lalmohan Babu's hand. Lalmohan Babu could only stare at him, completely taken aback.

Feluda slipped his little finger into the box and pushed at the small object, using a little force. It now came out like an obedient child. Feluda sniffed a couple of times and said, 'Araldite. Someone used Araldite on this piece of betel-nut. I wonder why—? Topshe, shut the door.' There were footsteps outside in the corridor. I did shut the door, but not before I had caught a glimpse of the man who went past our compartment. It was the same old man we had seen at the Jantar Mantar. He was still wearing the dark glasses and his ears were still plugged with cotton wool.

'Sh-h-h-h,' Feluda whistled.

He was gazing steadily at the little betel-nut that lay on his palm. I went forward for a closer look. It was clear that it was not a betel-nut at all. Some other object had been painted brown to camouflage it.

'I should have guessed,' said Feluda softly. 'I should have known a long time ago. Oh, what a fool I have been, Topshe!'

Feluda now lifted one of the glasses from its ring, poured a little water from our flask and dipped the betel-nut in it. The water began to turn a light brown as he gently rubbed the object. Then he wiped it with a handkerchief and put it back on his palm.

The betel-nut had disappeared. In its place was a beautifully cut, brilliant stone. From the way it glittered even in our semi-dark compartment, I could tell it was a diamond. And it was pretty obvious that none of us had seen such a large one ever before. At least, Lalmohan Babu made no bones about it.

'Is that . . .' he gasped, 'a d-di-di. . .?'

Feluda closed his fist around the stone, went over to the door to lock it, then came back and said, 'We've already had warnings threatening our lives. Why are you talking of dying?'

'No, no, not d-dying. I mean, is that a diam-m-m-?'

'Very probably, or it wouldn't be chased so persistently. But mind you, I am no expert.'

'Well then, is it val-val-val-?'

'I'm afraid the value of diamonds is something I don't know much about. I can only make a rough guess. This one, I think, is in the region of twenty carats. So its value would certainly exceed half a million rupees.'

Lalmohan Babu gulped in silence. Feluda was still turning the stone between his fingers.

'How did Dhameeja get hold of something so precious?' I asked under my breath.

'I don't know, dear boy. All I know about Dhameeja is that he said he had an orchard and that he likes reading thrillers on trains.'

Lalmohan Babu, in the meantime, had recovered somewhat. 'Will this stone now go back to Dhameeja?' he asked.

'If we can be sure that it is indeed his, then certainly it will go back to him.'

'Does that mean you suspect it might actually belong to someone else?'

'Yes, but there are other questions that need to be answered. For instance, I don't know if people outside Bengal are in the habit of chewing chopped betel-nuts.'

'But if that is so—' I began.

'No. No more questions tonight, Topshe. This whole affair has taken another new turn. We have to take every step with extreme caution. I can't waste any more time chatting.'

Feluda took out his wallet, put the sparkling stone away safely, pulled the zip and climbed on to his berth. I knew he didn't want to be disturbed. Lalmohan Babu opened his mouth to speak, but I laid a finger against my lips to stop him. He glanced once at Feluda and then turned to me. 'I think I'll give up writing suspense thrillers,' he confided.

'Why?'

'The few things that have happened in the last couple of days . . . they're beyond one's imagination, aren't they? Haven't you heard the saying, truth is stronger than fiction?'

'Not stronger. I think the word is stranger.'

'Stranger?'

'Yes, meaning more . . . amazing. More curious.'

'Oh really? I thought a stranger was someone one hadn't met before. Oh no, no, I see what you mean. Strange, stranger, strangest . . .'

I decided to cheer him up. 'We found the diamond only because of you,' I told him. 'If you hadn't finished all the real betel-nuts, that diamond would have remained hidden forever.'

Lalmohan Babu grinned from ear to ear.

'You mean to say even I have made a little contribution to this great mystery? Heh, heh, heh, heh . . .' Then he thought for a minute and added, 'You know what I really think? I am sure your cousin knew about the diamond right from the start. Or how could we have survived two attempts to steal it from us?'

This made me think. The thief had not yet managed to lay his hands on the real stuff. Not even by breaking into our hotel room. That precious stone was still with us. This meant we were probably still being followed, and therefore, in constant danger.

And we wouldn't be safe even in Simla . . .

Heaven knows when I fell asleep. I woke suddenly in the middle of the night. It was totally dark in the compartment, which meant even Feluda had switched off the reading lamp and gone to sleep. Lalmohan Babu was sleeping on the lower berth opposite mine. I was about to switch on my own lamp to look at the time, when my eyes fell on the door. The curtain from our side was drawn partially over the frosted glass. But there was a gap, and on this gap fell the shadow of a man.

What was he doing there? It took me a few seconds to realize he was actually trying to turn the handle of the door. I knew the door was locked and would not yield to pressure from outside; but even so, I began to feel breathless with fear.

How long the man would have persisted, it is difficult to say. But, only a few seconds later, Lalmohan Babu shouted 'Boomerang!' in his sleep, and the shadow disappeared.

I realized that even in the cool night air, I had broken into a cold sweat.

CHAPTER 8

I had seen snow-capped mountains before—
Kanchenjunga in Darjeeling and the top of Annapurna
from a plane; and certainly I had seen snow in films.
But nothing had startled me as much as what I saw in
Simla. If it wasn't for other Indians strolling on the
streets, I could have sworn we were in a foreign country.

'This town was built by the British, like Darjeeling,'
Feluda told me, 'so it does have the appearance of a
foreign city. One Lt. Ross built a wooden cottage here
in 1819 for himself. That was the beginning. Soon, the
British turned this into their summer capital, since in
the summer months life on the plains became pretty
uncomfortable.'

We had taken a metre gauge train at Kalka to reach
Simla. Nothing remarkable happened on the way,
although I noticed that the old man with the earplugs

travelled on the same train and checked in at the Clarkes just like us. Since the main season had not yet started, there were plenty of rooms available and Lalmohan Babu, too, found one at the Clarkes without any problem.

Feluda went looking for a post office soon after checking in. I offered to go with him, but he said someone should stay behind to guard the new attaché case; so Lalmohan Babu and I remained at the hotel. Feluda hadn't made a single remark on the snow or the beautiful town. Lalmohan Babu, on the other hand, appeared to be totally overwhelmed. Everything he saw struck him as 'fanastatic'. When I pointed out that the word was 'fantastic', he said airily that the speed with which he read English was so remarkable that not often did he find the time to look at the words carefully. Besides, there were a number of other questions he wanted answered—was it possible to find polar bears in Simla, did the Aurora Borealis appear here, did the Eskimos use the same snow to build their ilgoos (at which point I had to correct him again and say that it was igloos the Eskimos built, not ilgoos). The man was unstoppable.

The Clarkes Hotel stood on a slope. A veranda ran by the side of its second floor, which led to the street. The manager's room, the lounge, as well as our own rooms, were all on the second floor. Wooden stairs ran down to the first floor where there were more rooms and the dining-hall.

Feluda got delayed on his way back, so it was past 2 p.m. by the time we finished our lunch. A band was playing in one corner of the dining-hall. Lalmohan Babu called it a concert. The old man with the earplugs was also having lunch in the same room, as were three foreigners—two men and a woman. I had seen a man with dark glasses and a pointed beard leave the room when we came in. It did not appear as though there was anyone else in the hotel apart from these people and ourselves.

'We are going to see Mr Dhameeja today, aren't we?' I asked, slowly sipping the hot soup.

'Yes, at four o'clock. We needn't leave before three,' Feluda replied.

'Where exactly does he live?'

'The Wildflower Hall is on the way to Kufri. Eight miles from here.'

'Why should it take an hour to get there?'

'Most of the way is snowed under. The car might skid if we try to do anything other than crawl.' Then Feluda said to Lalmohan Babu, 'Wear all your warm clothes. This place we're going to is a thousand feet higher than Simla. The snow there is a lot worse.'

Lalmohan Babu put a spoonful of soup into his mouth, slurping noisily, and asked, 'Is a sherpa going to accompany us?'

I nearly burst out laughing, but Feluda kept a straight face. 'No,' he said seriously, 'there is actually a road that leads up there. We'll be going in a car.'

We finished our soup and were waiting for the next course, when Feluda spoke again. 'What happened to your weapon?' he asked Lalmohan Babu.

'I have it with me,' Lalmohan Babu replied, chewing a bread stick, 'haven't had the chance to show it to you, have I?'

'What is it?'

'A boomerang.'

Ah, that made sense. I had been wondering why he had shouted 'boomerang!' in his sleep.

'Where did you get a thing like that?'

'An Australian was selling some of his stuff. He had put an advertisement in the paper. There were many other interesting things, but I couldn't resist this one. I have heard that if you can throw it correctly, it would hit your target and return to you.'

'No, that's not quite true. It would come back to you only if it misses the target, not if it hits it.'

'Well yes, you may be right. But let me tell you one thing. It's damn difficult to throw it. I tried from my terrace, and it went and broke a flower pot on the balcony of the house opposite. Thank goodness, those people knew me and were kind enough to return my weapon without making a fuss about their flower pot.'

'Please don't forget to take it with you today.'

Lalmohan Babu's eyes began to shine with excitement.

'Are you expecting trouble?'

'Well, I can't guarantee anything, can I? After all, whoever has been trying to steal that diamond hasn't yet got it, has he?' Feluda spoke lightly, but I could see he was not totally easy in his mind.

At five to three, a blue Ambassador drove up and stopped before the main entrance. 'Here's our taxi,' said Feluda and stood up. Lalmohan Babu and I followed suit. The driver was a local man, young and well built.

Feluda joined him on the front seat, clutching Mr Dhameeja's (fake) attaché case. Jatayu and I sat at the back. The boomerang was hidden inside Jatayu's voluminous overcoat. I had taken a good look at it. It was made of wood and looked a bit like the bottom half of a hockey stick, although it was a lot thinner and smoother.

The sky had started to turn grey and the temperature dropped appreciably. But the clouds were not very heavy, so it did not seem as though it might rain. We left for the Wildflower Hall on the dot of 3 p.m.

Our hotel was in the main town. We hadn't had the chance to go out of the hotel since our arrival. The true spirit of the cold, sombre, snow-covered mountains struck me only when our car left the town and began its journey along a quiet, narrow path.

The mountains rose on one side, on the other was a deep ravine. The road was wide enough to allow another car to squeeze past, but that was just about all it could do. A thick pine forest grew on the mountains.

The first four miles were covered at a reasonable speed since the snow on the road was almost negligible. Through the pine trees, I could catch glimpses of heavier snow on the mountains at a distance; but, soon, the snow on the road we were on grew very much thicker. Feluda was right.

We had to reduce our speed and crawl carefully, following the tyre marks of cars that had preceded us. The ground was so slippery that, at times, the car failed to move forward, its wheels spinning furiously.

The tip of my nose and my ears began to feel icy.

Lalmohan Babu told me at one point that his ears were ringing. Five minutes later he said he had a blocked nose. I paid little attention. The last thing I was worried about was how my body would cope with the cold. All I could do was look around me and wonder at this remarkable place. Did man indeed live here? Wasn't this a corner nature had created only for animals and birds and insects that lived in snowy mountains? Shouldn't this stay unspoilt and untouched by the human hand? But no, the road we were travelling on had been built by man, other cars had driven on the same road and, no doubt, others would follow. In fact, if this wonderful place had not already been discovered by man, I would not be here today.

The unmarred strange whiteness ended abruptly about twenty minutes later, with a black wooden board by the side of the road that proclaimed in white letters: Wildflower Hall. I had not expected our journey to end so peacefully.

A little later we came upon a gate with The Nook written on it. Our car turned right and drove through this gate. A long driveway led to a large, old-fashioned bungalow, very obviously built during British times. Its roof and parapets were covered with a thick layer of snow. Its occupant had to be a pukka sahib, or he wouldn't live in a place like this.

Our taxi drew up under the portico. A man in a uniform came out and took Feluda's card. A minute later, the owner of the house came out himself with an outstretched arm.

'Good afternoon, Mr Mitter. I must say I am most impressed by your punctuality. Do come in, please.'

Mr Dhameeja might have been an Englishman. His diction was flawless. His appearance fitted Mr Lahiri's description. Feluda introduced me and Lalmohan Babu, and then we all went in. The floor was wooden, as were the walls of the huge drawing-room. A fire crackled in the fireplace.

Feluda handed over the blue attaché case before he sat down. The smile on Mr Dhameeja's face did not falter. Our attempt at deception was thus rewarded with complete success.

'Thank you so much. I've got Mr Lahiri's case and kept it handy.'

'Please check the contents in your case,' said Feluda with a slight smile.

'If you say so,' replied Mr Dhameeja, laughing, and opened the case. Then he ran his eyes over the items we had so carefully placed in it and said, 'Yes, everything's fine, except that these newspapers are not mine.'

'Not yours?' asked Feluda, retrieving the two English dailies.

'No, and neither is this.'

Mr Dhameeja returned the box of betel-nuts, which had been filled at the Kalka railway station. 'Oh, I see,' said Feluda. 'Those must have got there by mistake.'

Well, at least it proved that Mr Dhameeja knew nothing about the diamond. But, in that case, how did the box get inside the attaché case?

'And here is Mr Lahiri's case,' said Mr Dhameeja, picking up an identical attaché case from a side table and handing it over to Feluda. 'May I,' he added, 'make the same request? Please check its contents.'

'There's really only one thing Mr Lahiri is interested in. A bottle of enterovioform tablets.'

'Yes, it's there.'

' . . . And, a manuscript?'

'Manuscript?'

Feluda had opened the case. A brief glance even from a distance told me that there was not even a scrap of paper in it, let alone a whole manuscript.

Feluda was frowning deeply, staring into the open attaché. 'What manuscript are you talking about?' asked Mr Dhameeja.

Feluda said nothing. I could see what a difficult position he was in; either Mr Dhameeja had to be accused of stealing, or we had to take our leave politely, without Shambhucharan's tale of Tibet.

Mercifully, Mr Dhameeja continued to speak. 'I am very sorry, Mr Mitter, but that attaché case now contains exactly what I found in it when I opened it in my room in the Grand Hotel. I searched it thoroughly in the hope of finding its owner's address. But there was nothing, and certainly not a manuscript. On my return to Simla, I kept it locked in my own cupboard. Not for a second did anyone else touch it. I can guarantee that.'

After a speech like that, there was very little that Feluda could do. He rose to his feet and said with a slightly embarrassed air, 'It must be my mistake, then. Please don't mind, Mr Dhameeja. Thank you very much for your help. We should perhaps now be making a move.'

'Why? Allow me at least to offer you a cup of tea. Or would you prefer coffee?'

'No, no, nothing, thank you. It's getting late. We

really ought to go. Good-bye.'

We came out of the bungalow and got into our taxi. I was feeling even more confused. Where could the manuscript have disappeared? Naresh Pakrashi had told us that he didn't see Mr Lahiri read on the train. Was that the truth?

Had Dinanath Lahiri simply told us a pack of lies?

CHAPTER 9

It grew darker soon after we left. But it was only 4.25
p.m. Surely the sun wasn't setting already? I looked
at the sky, and found the reason. The light grey clouds
had turned into heavy, black ones. Please God, don't
let it rain. The road was already slippery. Since we were
now going to go downhill, the chances of skidding were
greater. The only good thing was that traffic was
virtually nonexistent, so there was no fear of crashing
into another car.

Feluda was sitting next to the driver. I couldn't see
his face, but could tell that he was still frowning. And I
also knew what he was thinking. Either Dinanath Babu
or Mr Dhameeja had lied to us. Mr Dhameeja's living-
room had been full of books. Perhaps he knew the
name of Shambhucharan. An account of a visit to Tibet
fifty years ago—and that, too, written in English—might

well have been a temptation. It was not totally impossible, was it? But if the manuscript was with Mr Dhameeja, how on earth would Feluda ever retrieve it?

Clearly, there were two mysteries now. One involved the diamond, and the other the missing manuscript. What if such a terrible tangle proved too much to unravel, even for Feluda?

The temperature had dropped further. I could see my breath condensing all the time. Lalmohan Babu undid the top button of his overcoat, slipped his hand in and said, 'Even the boomerang feels stone cold. It comes from a warm country, doesn't it? I hope it'll work here in this climate.' I opened my mouth to tell him there were places in Australia where it snowed, but had to shut it. Our car had come to a complete halt. And the reason was simple. A black Ambassador blocked our way. About a hundred yards away, diagonally across the road, stood this other car, making it impossible for us to proceed.

When the loud blowing of our horn did not help, it became obvious that something was wrong. The driver of the other car was nowhere in sight.

Feluda placed a hand on the steering wheel and quietly told the driver to move his car to one side, closer to the hill. The driver did this without a word. Then all four of us got out and stepped on to the slushy path.

Everything was very quiet. Not even the twitter of a bird broke the eerie silence. What was most puzzling was that there was neither a driver nor a passenger in the black car. Who would place a car across the road like that and then abandon it totally?

We were making our way very cautiously along

the tyre marks on the snow, when a sudden splashing noise made Lalmohan Babu give a violent start, stumble and go sprawling on the snow. He landed flat on his face. I knew the noise had been caused by a chunk of thawing ice that had dislodged itself from a branch. In the total silence of the surroundings, it did sound as loud as a pistol shot. Feluda and I pulled Lalmohan Babu up to his feet and we resumed walking.

A few yards later, I realized I had been wrong. There was indeed a figure sitting in the car, in the driver's seat. 'I know this man,' said our driver, Harbilas, peering carefully, 'he is a taxi driver like me. And this taxi is his own. He's called Arvind. But . . . but . . . I think he's unconscious, or perhaps . . . dead?'

Feluda's right hand automatically made its way to his pocket. I knew he was clutching his revolver.

Splash!

Another chunk of ice fell, a lot closer this time. Lalmohan Babu started again, but managed to stop himself from stumbling. In the next instant, however, a completely unexpected ear-splitting noise made him lose control and he went rolling on the snow once more. This time, it was a pistol shot.

The bullet hit the ground less than ten yards ahead of us, making the snow spray up in the air. Feluda had pulled me aside the moment the shot was fired, and we had both thrown ourselves on the ground. Lalmohan Babu came rolling half a second later. The driver, too, had jumped behind the car. Although young and strong, clearly he had never had to cope with such a situation before.

The sound of the shot echoed among the hills.

Someone hiding in the pine forest had fired at us. Presumably, he couldn't see us any more for we were shielded by the black Ambassador.

Lying prostrate on the ground, I tried to come to terms with this new development. Something cold and wet was tickling the back of my neck. I turned my head a few degrees and realized what it was. A fine white curtain of snow had been thrown down from the sky. Even in such a moment of danger, I couldn't help staring—fascinated—at the little flakes that fell like cotton fluff. For the first time in my life, I discovered falling snow made no noise at all. Lalmohan Babu looked as though he was about to make a remark, but one gesture from Feluda made him change his mind.

At this precise moment, the silence was shattered once more, but not by a pistol shot, or a chunk of ice, or the sound of wheels turning in the slippery snow. This time, we heard the voice of a man.

'Mr Mitter!'

Who was this? Why did the voice sound vaguely familiar?

'Listen carefully, Mr Mitter,' it went on. 'You must have realized by now that I have got you where I want you. So don't try any clever tricks. It's not going to work and, in fact, your lives may be in danger.'

It was some time before the final echo of the words died down. Then the man spoke again.

'I want only one thing from you, Mr Mitter.'

'What is it?' Feluda shouted back.

'Come out from where you're hiding. I would like to see you, although you couldn't see me even if you tried. I will answer your question when you come out.'

For a few minutes, I had been aware of a strange noise in my immediate vicinity. At first I thought it was coming from inside the car. Now I turned my head and realized it was simply the sound of Lalmohan Babu's chattering teeth.

Feluda rose to his feet and slowly walked over to the other side of the car, without uttering a word. Perhaps he knew under the circumstances, it was best to do as he was told. Never before had I seen him grapple with such a difficult situation.

'I hope,' said the voice, 'that your three companions realize that a single move from them would simply spell disaster.'

'Kindly tell me what you want,' said Feluda.

I could see him standing from behind one of the wheels. He was looking up at the mountain. In front of him lay a wide expanse of snow. The pine forest started at some distance.

'Take out your revolver,' commanded the voice. Feluda obeyed.

'Throw it across on the slope.' Feluda did.

'Do you have the Kodak container?'

'Yes.'

'Show it to me.'

Feluda took out the yellow container from his pocket and raised it.

'Now show me the stone you found in it.'

Feluda slipped his hand into the pocket of his jacket. Then he brought it out and held it high once more, holding a small object between his thumb and forefinger.

No one spoke for a few seconds. No doubt the

man was trying to take a good look at the diamond.
Did he have binoculars, I wondered.

'All right,' the voice came back. 'Now put that stone
back into its container and place it on that large grey
boulder by the side of the road. Then you must return
straight to Simla. If you think . . . '

Feluda cut him short.

'You really want this stone, don't you?' he asked.

'For God's sake, do I have to spell it out?' the voice
retorted sharply.

'Well then, here it is!'

Feluda swung his arm and threw the stone in the
direction of the forest. This was followed by a breath-
taking sequence of events.

Our invisible adversary threw himself out of his
hiding place in an attempt to catch the diamond, but
fell on a slab of half-frozen snow. In the next instant,
he lost his foothold and was rolling down the hill like
a giant snowball. He finally came to rest near the snow-
covered nullah that ran alongside the road. By this time,
the pistol and binoculars had dropped from his hands.
A pair of dark glasses and a pointed beard lay not far
from these.

There was no point in our hiding any more. The
three of us leapt to our feet and ran forward to join
Feluda. I had expected the other man to be at least
unconscious, if not dead. He had slipped from a
considerable height at enormous speed. But, to my
surprise, I found him lying flat on his back, glaring
malevolently at Feluda and breathing deeply.

It was easy enough now to understand why his
voice had sounded familiar. The figure stretched out

on the snow was none other than the unsuccessful film star, Amar Kumar, alias Prabeer Lahiri, Dinanath Babu's nephew.

Feluda spoke with ice in his voice. 'You do realize, don't you, that the tables have turned? So stop playing this game and let's hear what you have to say.'

Prabeer Lahiri did not reply. He continued to lie on his back, snow drifting down on his upturned face, gazing steadily at Feluda.

Nothing was as yet clear to me, but I hoped Prabeer Babu would throw some light on the mystery. But still he said nothing.

'Very well,' said Feluda, 'if you will not open your mouth, allow me to do the talking. Pray tell me if I get anything wrong. You had got the diamond from that Nepali box, hadn't you? It was possibly the same jewel that the Rana of Nepal had given to Shambhucharan as a token of his gratitude. That box, in fact, must have been Shambhucharan's property; and he must have left it before his death with his friend, Satinath Lahiri. Satinath brought it back to India with him, but was unable to tell anyone about the diamond, presumably because by the time he returned, he was seriously ill. You found it only a few days ago purely by chance. Then you painted it brown and kept it together with chopped betel-nuts in that empty film container. When your uncle gave you the Air-India attaché case, you thought it would be perfectly safe to hide your diamond in it. But what you didn't foresee was that only a day later, the case would make its way from your room to mine. You eavesdropped, didn't you, when your uncle was talking to us that evening in your house? So you decided to steal it from me. When the telephone call from a fictitious Mr Puri and the efforts of your hired hooligans failed, you chased us to Delhi. But even that didn't work, did it? You took a very great risk by breaking into our room in the hotel, but the diamond still eluded your grasp. There was really only one thing you could do after that. You followed us to Simla and planned this magnificent fiasco.'

Feluda stopped. We were all standing round, staring at him, totally fascinated.

'Tell me, Mr Lahiri, is any of this untrue?'

The look in Prabeer Lahiri's eyes underwent a swift change. His eyes glittered and his lips spread in a cunning smile. 'What are you talking about, Mr Mitter?' he asked almost gleefully. 'What diamond? I know nothing about this!'

My heart missed a beat. The diamond was lost in the snow. Perhaps forever. How could Feluda prove—?

'Why, Mr Lahiri,' Feluda said softly, 'are you not acquainted with this little gem?'

We started again. Feluda had slipped his hand into a different pocket and brought out another stone. Even in the fading light from the overcast sky, it winked merrily.

'That little stone that's buried in the snow was something I bought this morning at the Miller Gem Company in Simla. Do you know how much I spent on it? Five rupees. This one is the real . . . '

He couldn't finish. Prabeer Lahiri sprang up like a tiger and jumped on Feluda, snatching the diamond from his hand.

Clang!

This time, Feluda, too, gave a start. This unexpected noise was simply the result of Lalmohan Babu's boomerang hitting Prabeer Lahiri's head. He sank down on the snow again, unconscious. The diamond returned to Feluda.

'Thank you, Lalmohan Babu.'

But it was doubtful whether Lalmohan Babu heard the words for he was staring, dumbfounded, at the boomerang that had shot out in the air from his own right hand and found its mark so accurately.

CHAPTER 10

The budding film star, Amar Kumar, was now a sorry sight. He had made a full confession in the car on the way back to Simla. This was made easier by the revolver in Feluda's hand, which he had recovered soon after the drama ended. It had not taken Prabeer Babu long to come round. Lalmohan Babu, having thrown the boomerang at him, had made an attempt at nursing him by scooping up a handful of snow and plastering his head with it. I cannot tell if it helped in any way, but he opened his eyes soon enough.

The driver called Arvind had also regained consciousness and was, reportedly, feeling better. He had, at first, been offered money to join Prabeer Lahiri. But when he refused to be tempted, Prabeer Babu lost his patience and simply knocked him out.

Things had started to go wrong for Prabeer Lahiri

ever since he was dropped from the film. It had been a long-cherished dream that he would be a famous film star one day, living in luxury, chased by thousands of admirers. When his voice let him down and this dream was shattered, Prabeer Lahiri, in a manner of speaking, lost his head.

He had to get what he wanted. If it was not possible to fulfil his dream by fair means, he was prepared to adopt unfair ones. By a strange twist of fate, the Nepali box fell into his hands, like manna from heaven. In it he found a stone beautifully cut and sparkling bright. When he had it valued, it took his breath away; and his plans took a different shape. He would produce his own film, he decided, and take the lead role. No one— but no one—could have him dropped. What followed this decision was now history.

We handed him over to the Himachal Pradesh state police. It turned out that Feluda's suspicions had fallen on Prabeer Babu as soon as we had found the diamond. So he had called Dinanath Lahiri immediately on arrival in Simla, and asked him to join us. Mr Lahiri was expected to reach Simla the next day. It would then be up to him to decide what should be done with his nephew. The diamond would probably return to Dinanath Babu, since it had been found amongst his uncle's belongings.

'That's all very well,' I said, after Feluda explained the whole story, 'but what about Shambhucharan's travelogue?'

'That,' said Feluda, 'is mystery number two. You've heard of double-barrelled guns, haven't you? This one's a double-barrelled mystery.'

'But are we anywhere near finding its solution?'

'Yes, my dear boy, yes. Thanks to the newspapers and that glass of water.'

Feluda's words sounded no less mysterious, so I decided not to probe any further. He, too, said nothing more.

We returned to the hotel without any other excitement on the way. A few minutes later, we were seated on the open terrace of the hotel under a colourful canopy, sipping hot chocolate. Seven other tables stood on the terrace. Two Japanese men sat at the next one and, at some distance, sat the old man who had travelled with us from Delhi. He had removed the cotton wool from his ears.

The sky was now clear, but the evening light was fading rather quickly. The main city of Simla lay among the eastern hills. I could see its streets and houses being lit up one by one.

Lalmohan Babu had been very quiet, lost in his thoughts. Now he took a long sip of his chocolate and said, 'Perhaps it is true that there is an underlying current of viciousness in the mind of every human being. Don't you agree, Felu Babu? When one blow from my boomerang made that man spin and fall, I felt so . . . excited. Even pleased. It's strange!'

'Man descended from monkeys,' Feluda remarked. 'You knew that, didn't you? Well, a modern theory now says that it was really a special breed in Africa that was man's ancestor. It's well known for its killer instinct. So, if you are feeling pleased about having hit Prabeer

Lahiri, your ancestors are to blame.'

An interesting theory, no doubt. But I was in no mood to discuss monkeys. My mind kept going back to Shambhucharan. Where was his manuscript? Who had got it? Or could it be that no one did, and the whole thing was a lie? But why should anyone tell such a lie?

I had to speak.

'Feluda,' I blurted out, 'who is the liar? Dhameeja or Dinanath Babu?'

'Neither.'

'You mean the manuscript does exist?'

'Yes, but whether we'll ever get it back is extremely doubtful.' Feluda sounded grave.

'Do you happen to know,' I asked tentatively, 'who has got it?'

'Yes, I do. It's all quite clear to me now. But the man who has it is so remarkably clever that it would be very difficult indeed to prove anything against him. To tell you the truth, he almost managed to hoodwink me.'

'Almost?' The word pleased me for I would have hated to think Feluda had been totally fooled by anyone.

'Mitter sahib!'

This came from a bearer who was standing near the door, glancing around uncertainly.

'Here!' Feluda shouted, waving. The bearer made his way to our table, clutching a brown parcel.

'Someone left this for you in the manager's room,' he said.

Feluda's name was written on it in large bold letters: MR P. C. MITTER, CLARKES HOTEL.

Feluda's expression had changed the minute the parcel was handed to him. Now he opened it swiftly and exclaimed, 'What! Where did this come from?'

A familiar smell came from the parcel. Feluda held up its content. I stared at an ancient notebook, the kind that was impossible to find nowadays. The front page had these words written on it in a very neat hand:

A Bengalee in Lamaland
Shambhucharan Bose
June 1917

'Good heavens! It's that famous manusprint!' said Lalmohan Babu.

I did not bother to correct him. I could only look dumbly at Feluda, who was staring straight at something specific. I turned my gaze in the same direction. The two Japanese had gone. There was only one other person left on the terrace, apart from ourselves. It was the same old man we had seen so many times before. He was still wearing a cap and dark glasses. Feluda was looking straight at him.

The man rose to his feet and walked over to our table. Then he took off his glasses and his cap. Yes, he certainly seemed familiar. But there was something odd . . . something missing . . . what had I seen before . . . ?

'Aren't you going to wear your false teeth?' Feluda asked.

'Certainly.'

The man took out a set of false teeth from his pocket and slipped it into his mouth. Instantly, his hollowed cheeks filled out, his jaw became firm and he began to look ten years younger. And it was easy to recognize him.

This was none other than that supremely irritable man we had visited in Lansdowne Road, Mr Naresh Chandra Pakrashi.

'When did you get the dentures made?' asked Feluda.

'I had ordered them a while ago. But they were delivered the day after I returned to Calcutta from Delhi.'

That explained why Dinanath Babu had thought him old. He had not worn his dentures on the train. But he had started using them by the time we met him in his house.

'I had guessed from the start that the attaché cases had been exchanged deliberately,' Feluda told him. 'I knew it was no accident. But what I did not know— and it took me a long time to figure that one out—was that you were responsible.'

'That is natural enough,' Mr Pakrashi replied calmly. 'You must have realized that I am no fool.'

'No, most certainly you are not. But do you know where you went wrong? You shouldn't have put those newspapers in Mr Dhameeja's attaché case. I know why you did it, though. Dinanath Lahiri's case was heavier than Dhameeja's because it had this notebook in it. So you stuffed the newspapers in Dhameeja's case, so that its weight became more or less the same as Dinanath's. When Dinanath Babu picked it up, naturally he noticed nothing unusual. But people don't normally bother to pack their cases with papers they've read on the train, do they?'

'You're right. But then, you are more intelligent than most. Not many would have picked that up.'

'I have a question to ask,' Feluda continued.

'Everyone, with the sole exception of yourself, slept well that night, didn't they?'

'Hmm . . . yes, you might say that.'

'And yet, Dinanath Lahiri says he cannot sleep in a moving train. Did you drug him?'

'Right.'

'By crushing a pill and pouring it into a glass of water?'

'Yes. I always carry my sleeping pills with me. Everyone had been given a glass of water when dinner was served, and two of the passengers went to wash their hands. Only Dhameeja didn't.'

'Does that mean you couldn't tamper with Mr Dhameeja's drinking water?'

'No, and as a result of that I couldn't do a thing during the night. At six in the morning, Dhameeja got up to have a shave and then went to the bathroom. I did what I had to do before he came back. Lahiri and the other one were still fast asleep.'

'I see. You took one hell of a risk, didn't you, with Dhameeja actually in the compartment, when you poured the pill into Dinanath's water?'

'I was lucky. He didn't even glance at me.'

'Yes, lucky you certainly were. But, later, you did something that gave you away. It was a clever move, no doubt, but what made you offer me money even after you had got hold of Shambhucharan's manuscript?'

Mr Pakrashi burst out laughing, but said nothing.

'That phone call in Calcutta and that piece of paper in Delhi . . . you were behind both, weren't you?'

'Yes, of course. I did not want you to go to Simla— at least, not at first. I knew a man like you would tear apart my perfect crime. So I rang your house and even slipped a written threat into your friend's pocket when I found him sitting next to me in the plane. But then . . . slowly, I began to change my mind. By the time I reached Simla, I was convinced I should return the stolen property to you.'

'Why?'

'Because if you went back without the manuscript, you yourself might have been under suspicion. I did not want that to happen. I have come to appreciate you and your methods in these few days, you see.'

'Thank you, Mr Pakrashi. One more question.'

'Yes?'

'You made a duplicate copy of the whole manuscript before returning it to me, didn't you?'

All the colour from Mr Pakrashi's face receded instantly. Feluda had played his trump card.

'When we went to your house, you were typing something. It was the stuff in this notebook, wasn't it? You were typing every word in it.'

'But . . . you . . . '

'There was a funny smell in your room, the same as the smell in Shambhucharan's old Nepali box. And now I can see that this notebook has it, too.'

'But the copy—'

'Let me finish. Shambhucharan died in 1921. Fifty-one years ago. That means the fifty-year copyright period was over a year ago. So anyone can now have it printed, right?'

'Of course!' Mr Pakrashi shouted, displaying signs of agitation. 'Are you trying to tell me I did wrong? Never! It's an extraordinary tale, I tell you. Dinanath wouldn't have known its value, nor would he have had it published. I am going to print it now, and no one can stop me.'

'Oh, sure. No one can stop you, Mr Pakrashi, but what's wrong with a bit of healthy competition?'

'Competition? What do you mean?'

Feluda's famous lopsided smile peeped out. He stretched his right hand towards Mr Pakrashi.

'Meet your rival, Naresh Babu,' he said. 'When Dinanath Lahiri arrives tomorrow, I shall not ask for my fees with regard to this mysterious case. All I do want from him is this old notebook. And I happen to know a few publishers who might be interested. Now do you begin to see what I mean?'

Naresh Pakrashi glared in silence.

Lalmohan Babu, however, suddenly found his voice, and uttered one word, without any apparent rhyme or reason.

'Boomerang!' he yelled.